A Capitol Crime

Read all the mysteries in the
NANCY DREW DIARIES

❧

Nancy Drew DIARIES™

A Capitol Crime

#22

CAROLYN KEENE

Aladdin
NEW YORK LONDON TORONTO SYDNEY NEW DELHI

ALADDIN

An imprint of Simon & Schuster Children's Publishing Division
1230 Avenue of the Americas, New York, New York 10020
First Aladdin hardcover edition May 2021
Text copyright © 2021 by Simon & Schuster, Inc.
Jacket illustration copyright © 2021 by Erin McGuire
Also available in an Aladdin paperback edition.
All rights reserved, including the right of reproduction in whole or in part in any form.
ALADDIN and related logo are registered trademarks of Simon & Schuster, Inc.
NANCY DREW, NANCY DREW DIARIES, and related logo are
trademarks of Simon & Schuster, Inc.
For information about special discounts for bulk purchases, please contact
Simon & Schuster Special Sales at 1-866-506-1949 or business@simonandschuster.com.
The Simon & Schuster Speakers Bureau can bring authors to your live event.
For more information or to book an event contact the Simon & Schuster Speakers Bureau
at 1-866-248-3049 or visit our website at www.simonspeakers.com.
Series designed by Karin Paprocki
Jacket designed by Heather Palisi
Interior designed by Mike Rosamilia
The text of this book was set in Adobe Caslon Pro.
Manufactured in the United States of America 0421 FFG
2 4 6 8 10 9 7 5 3 1
Library of Congress Cataloging-in-Publication Data
Names: Keene, Carolyn, author.
Title: A Capitol crime / by Carolyn Keene.
Description: New York : Aladdin, 2021. | Series: Nancy Drew diaries ; 22 | Audience: Ages 8 to 12. |
Summary: "Nancy investigates her father's disappearance in Washington, DC,
in the twenty-second book of the Nancy Drew Diaries"— Provided by publisher.
Identifiers: LCCN 2020056499 (print) | LCCN 2020056500 (ebook) |
ISBN 9781534444393 (hardcover) | ISBN 9781534444386 (paperback) |
ISBN 9781534444409 (ebook)
Subjects: CYAC: Missing persons—Fiction. |
Washington (D.C.)—Fiction. | Mystery and detective stories.
Classification: LCC PZ7.K23 Car 2021 (print) | LCC PZ7.K23 (ebook) | DDC [Fic]—dc23
LC record available at https://lccn.loc.gov/2020056499
LC ebook record available at https://lccn.loc.gov/2020056500

Contents

Dear Diary,

DAD WAS OUT OF TOWN AT A CONFERENCE and Hannah had to go take care of her sister, so I had the house to myself. I was looking forward to a few days of relaxing and catching up with Bess and George. Instead I found myself jetting off to our nation's capital for my most personal case yet. . . .

~

CHAPTER ONE

A Bad Feeling

"SERIOUSLY, GEORGE?" I ASKED, SETTING my fork down with a clang. "Another photo?"

"That one didn't capture just how smooth these mashed potatoes are!" George said as she snapped yet another picture with the camera on her phone.

I sighed as she scowled at her latest effort before lifting the phone again. I was starving and couldn't wait to eat, but George is one of my best friends, and I know her quirks well. When George is focused on something, she gets in a zone, becoming oblivious to anything other than her current obsession. I was just going to have to wait until she got a photo she was satisfied with.

Next to me, Bess, my other best friend and George's cousin, gave me a sympathetic smile. She knows how George gets too.

Finally George looked up at us. "All right. Photographed, filtered, and shared." She held up the photo she'd posted. I couldn't argue with the results. The image was flawless and the food looked delicious. "Sorry that took so long," George said through a mouthful of potato. "I wanted to do the food justice. When Hannah gets back, I'll show her how many likes it got. I keep telling her if she set up an Instagram account for her food, she'd get a huge following. She'd be a star!"

My frown softened. "That's actually really nice of you."

Hannah Gruen's our housekeeper. She's been taking care of me and my dad since my mom died when I was three. She was supposed to stay with me while Dad was away at a lawyer's conference in Washington,

DC, but her sister broke her leg, so Hannah had had to hop on a last-minute flight to go and take care of her. When George and Bess found out, they were worried about me getting lonely, so they offered to come stay for a few days. The plan was to make it a real girls' weekend.

Before she'd left, Hannah had whipped up some of our favorite foods: mashed potatoes for George, oven-fried chicken for Bess, and a tomato-and-mozzarella salad for me.

"So what exactly is this conference your dad's at, Nancy?" Bess asked.

"It happens every year. Lawyers from all around the country get together and talk about updates to certain laws. There are panels and speeches and parti—"

George's phone buzzed loudly against the table, cutting me off. Without thinking, she reached for it and tapped the screen.

I felt my stomach drop. The three of us had been so busy recently, we'd barely been able to spend any time together. George had been working overtime at the Coffee Cabin, saving up for a new laptop. Bess had started dating a new guy named Teddy. And I'd been wrapped up consulting with the River Heights PD on a case.

I'm a detective. Usually I help find items that have been stolen or track down saboteurs, but sometimes the police ask me to provide a second pair of eyes on matters that are stumping them. This last one had been a doozy involving a car theft ring, and I had put in a lot of hours.

That's why I'd really been looking forward to the three of us spending time with one another and catching up, but if the last ten minutes had been anything to go by, George was going to be distracted by her phone the whole night.

Besides, we had a rule about this.

"No phones at the table, George!" I reminded her.

She pulled her hand back sheepishly. "I know. I'm sorry! I can't help it. It buzzes and I reach for it."

"You're like one of Pavlov's dogs, George!" Bess quipped.

"What's that supposed to mean?" asked George, crossing her arms.

"Pavlov did an experiment where he rang a bell every time he fed a group of dogs. Soon, they'd drool whenever they heard a bell. That's you when your phone buzzes."

"Rude! But accurate," she admitted much more quietly.

"Maybe I should lock your phone in my dad's safe," I suggested.

George's eyes widened. "Well, if you lock up mine, you'll need to lock up Bess's, too! She's been sneaking texts with Teddy under the table since we sat down."

I turned to Bess, eyebrow raised. She was bright red and could barely meet my gaze. Bess hates breaking the rules and is the politest, kindest person I've ever met. Still, it was clear from her expression that George was telling the truth.

"I'm sorry!" she said. "Our relationship is just so new, I didn't want him to think I was ghosting him."

I have to admit, I was a little surprised. Not that a boy

was interested in Bess—she's one of those people who can smile at a guy, and he's instantly smitten. Cashiers and waiters are pining for her all over town. And it's understandable. She's pretty, but more than that, I think they can sense her inherent kindness. No, what shocked me was how invested she seemed in this Teddy. Bess tends to keep her relationships pretty casual.

"What about you, Nancy?" George asked. "Are you telling me you haven't played any *Words with Friends* with Ned since we've been over?"

"No!" I answered firmly, but I had to admit, the thought had crossed my mind. Ned's my boyfriend, and we've been caught up in an epic *Words with Friends* battle for the past few months. He's ahead of me, but only by one game. And when we're in the middle of a close match, it can be hard to resist making a move, even if I'm tied up with something else. "To be fair," I said, "he's at his grandmother's and he doesn't have any service there."

George laughed. "See? Staying connected is just a way of life now. We shouldn't fight it." George loves anything techie. She's been coding since she was little, and she's always the first to buy the latest gadget. I don't have a problem with technology—it's definitely helped me solve more than one case—but I don't love it the way George does. And while I can momentarily get as caught up in social media as the next person, I like to take a break from it every once in a while.

"It's just that I really wanted tonight to be about us," I explained. "I've barely seen you two in ages. George, I'm sure you've had some memorable customers you want to vent about. And Bess, don't pretend that you don't want to tell us all about how great Teddy is."

"I *have* been kind of bursting to tell you about him," Bess admitted.

George leaned forward. "I don't know if the planets have been aligned in some weird way—you know I'm not into astrology stuff—but this week was a killer at work."

"But hearing about it isn't the same if we're all keeping one eye on our text messages or Instagram likes," I explained. "It's as if we're not really here."

George and Bess both nodded.

"You're right," Bess said.

George handed me her phone. "You probably *should* lock this up. . . ."

As soon as I had my fingers wrapped around the case, the phone buzzed in my hand. George made an exaggerated grimace. "Take it away, Nancy! It's killing me not to look!" She slumped down in her seat, pretending to be dead.

I giggled. "You're so ridiculous."

Without hesitating, Bess handed me her phone too. She has incredible self-control. "Really?" I asked.

She nodded, though it looked like it pained her.

"Wow. Teddy must be some guy," I said.

"He's really nice," Bess replied, blushing.

"And cute!" George added. "Don't forget who introduced you!"

Bess shook her head. "I'll never forget, because you'll never let me!"

"Hang on one second. Let me put away our phones, and then I want to hear all about him."

I ran down the hall to my dad's office and unlocked the safe. He'd never told me the combination, but I'd figured it out a long time ago based on a pattern I'd noticed in some of his other passwords. He likes to combine the numbers of dates that are significant to him. His phone password is my mom's birthday plus their wedding anniversary. Once, when I was home sick and bored, I tried my birthday plus his on the safe's lock, and it'd worked. People think being a detective is about finding clues, and that's a big part of it, but being good at recognizing patterns is key, and I'd learned pretty early on that people tend to be very consistent.

I popped open the door and dropped the phones on top of our passports and other important papers, then locked it up again.

The rest of the evening passed exactly how I'd hoped.

Bess told us all about Teddy. By the time she was listing his astrological sign (Libra), favorite color (blue), and favorite ice cream flavor (a tie between cookies and cream and pistachio), George and I were doubled over, laughing at how enamored our best friend had become.

Then George told us about the awful customers who'd come to the Coffee Cabin over the past week, and I cracked up at her impressions of a lady complaining that the coffee didn't taste organic.

"What about you, Nancy? How's the car-theft case going?" Bess asked.

"I was riding along with one of the officers when they pulled over one of the thieves!"

"Does that mean you were in a car chase?" George asked, bouncing up and down.

I shook my head. "The guy didn't even try to get away. He thought he had the perfect explanation for driving a car that wasn't his."

"Let me guess," Bess said. "He was borrowing it from a friend?"

"No, get this. He claimed he was reviewing cars for *Car and Driver* magazine."

"But it would be so easy to prove he was lying," George said.

I shrugged. "Not everyone is a criminal mastermind."

After we'd cleaned up the dishes, we all tried out the moisturizing masks that Bess had brought with her. We even convinced George to use one, and she hates all that primping and fussing. George is more the roll-out-of-bed-and-pull-on-some-clothes-from-the-floor type. She complained loudly at first, and I think the only reason she agreed was because neither Bess nor I could threaten her with photographic evidence, since our phones were locked up. Twenty minutes later, she couldn't stop marveling at how her skin glowed. I think if Bess hadn't stopped her, George would have camped out in front of the bathroom mirror for the rest of the night.

Once we managed to drag her away, we went back down to the kitchen and made ice cream sundaes while we argued about which movie to watch, then got into our pajamas, set up the air mattresses in the living room, and resolved to stay up to watch them all.

I fell asleep around two in the morning in the middle of *To All the Boys I've Loved Before* (Bess's pick).

It was a fantastic night. That's why I was surprised to wake up with a start several hours later with a sinking feeling in the pit of my stomach. I have learned to trust my instincts over the years, and right then, they were screaming that something was very wrong.

A movie I didn't recognize was playing, and George and Bess were asleep next to me. I turned off the TV and lay very still, listening carefully, but all I heard was the hum of the refrigerator and George's quiet snores.

I was pretty sure there wasn't an intruder in the house, but the feeling that something was off wasn't going away, so I reached for my phone to see if anything big had happened in the world. And then remembered I didn't have it with me. Slowly, careful not to wake George and Bess, I got up, padded to Dad's office, and unlocked the safe, then took out my phone and turned it on. Seventeen missed calls, all of them from my dad! The first one had come in at 8:23 the night before. My heart started racing and sweat coated my palms.

I took a deep breath. If something had happened to Dad, he'd need me calm and in control. I looked at the screen again. There was one voice mail, and it was two minutes long. My hand was trembling as I hit play.

Everything was muffled, as if Dad's phone was still in his pocket when he'd called. At first, I could only make out the sound of footsteps—two sets of them. I recognized one immediately as Dad's, but the other pair sounded quieter, like the person was smaller and a little behind him. A woman, maybe? I could hear Dad's breathing. It was shallow and fast. He was scared.

A new bolt of fear went through me. My dad didn't scare easily.

After a moment, I heard Dad say, "You don't ha—" and then there was something else, but the lining of his pocket rubbing against the speaker created too much noise to make out what. I replayed the message and turned the volume all the way up, pressing the phone as close to my ear as I could, but I still couldn't understand what else he'd said. Frustrated, I took a deep breath, trying to focus. Maybe Dad would stop walking and I'd be able to make out what was happening.

I heard more footsteps—it sounded like they were

going down stairs. Then I thought I heard a door open and shut, but I couldn't be sure.

When Dad spoke again, it was hard to hear exactly what he was saying, but it sounded like, "Where are you taking me?" And then nothing. The message just ended.

I called Dad's cell phone as I sprinted down the hall. The call rang and rang and rang, and then: "This is Carson Drew. Leave a message and I'll call you back as soon as I can."

"Dad! Call me! Let me know you're all right!" My voice sounded breathless and thin. I hung up as I reached the living room and threw on the lights.

George groaned as she rolled over, pulling the blanket over her head.

"George, Bess! Wake up! It's an emergency!"

Bess's eyes blinked open, and she focused on me, confused. "Nancy? What's happening?"

"Wake up!" I repeated, ripping the blanket from George's head.

"What's going on?" she complained, rubbing her eyes.

"I think my dad's been kidnapped!"

George and Bess both sat up abruptly. "WHAT?" they shrieked.

I held up the screen so they could see all the missed calls, then played the voice mail. They didn't have any more luck making out what Dad had said than I'd had.

"I know your dad probably took his laptop with him, but does he still have that old desktop?" George asked me, now wide awake.

I nodded. "In his office."

A few moments later George was settled behind his desk, typing rapidly and clicking links. "Your dad is a very smart man. He set up a Find My Phone account. Do you happen to know his password?"

"Of course. It's NancyD123. I know all his passwords."

George blinked. "Well, that's definitely not secure. I thought I taught your dad better."

Bess tapped the desk. "Focus, George! You can scold Mr. Drew once we know he's safe."

"Yeah, okay. Give me a second."

I let out a deep breath, waiting impatiently as the program ran. It felt like it was taking forever, but only a few seconds later, an address flashed on the screen.

Hands shaking, I typed it into the search engine on my phone. "That's the Adams Hotel, where the conference is being held. Dad's staying there."

"If his phone is at the hotel, maybe he's at the hotel too," George suggested.

"Yeah," Bess agreed. "Maybe this is all some kind of misunderstanding."

"Maybe . . . ," I said, but I wasn't convinced. What we could hear of the message was too weird, and seventeen calls was too many to be an accident.

I tapped his number again, hoping that this time he'd pick up and give me a completely boring explanation for what had happened. And then George, Bess, and I could go to Nick's Diner for french toast and laugh about this whole incident.

"This is Carson Drew. Leave—" I hung up. No french toast for us.

"Maybe he's still asleep," Bess offered, but without any conviction.

I shook my head. "It's after seven, and my dad wakes up at six on the dot every day. He's part man, part alarm clock."

Suddenly my phone buzzed in my hand with a number I didn't recognize.

"Hello?"

"Is this Nancy? Nancy Drew?" a man's voice said on the other end.

"Yes, this is she."

"My name's Jesse Wei. I'm friends with your father. We're both at the conference in DC."

"Is he okay?" I asked. I could hear my voice rising an octave. "Have you seen him?"

"That's why I'm calling. Carson's missing."

CHAPTER TWO

Doppelgänger

"WHAT DO YOU MEAN, 'MISSING'?" I ASKED, quickly putting my phone on speaker so Bess and George could hear what Mr. Wei was saying.

"Well, we were supposed to have breakfast an hour ago, but he never showed up. And you know your dad. He's never late. I called his phone and he didn't answer, so I went to his room and knocked to make sure he was okay—I was worried he might be sick or something—but he didn't answer. It's just not like him to stand someone up."

My breathing grew unsteady again. Noticing, Bess

squeezed my hand. Mr. Wei was right. If I had to pick one word to describe my dad, it would be "reliable." When he says he's going to be somewhere, he's there and on time. Even though he's a busy lawyer, Dad never missed a single ballet recital, tennis match, or parent-teacher conference.

"I asked around," Mr. Wei continued. "No one's seen him since the plenary yesterday evening."

"What's a plenary?" George asked.

"Oh, it just means a session everyone at the conference attends," Mr. Wei explained. "Most of the programming is panels or small group discussions."

"Got it," George replied with a nod.

"Anyway," Mr. Wei continued. "I know Carson hasn't been missing long enough to go to the police, but your dad's so proud of your detective work, Nancy. He's always talking about it. Hearing about your cases is a highlight of catching up with him. I'm sure he'll turn up with some perfectly logical explanation for where he's been, but I thought I should give you a call anyway."

"Yes, thank you so much for calling. I'm definitely going to get on this."

"There's a flight in an hour and a half," George said, from behind my dad's computer. "If we hurry, we can just make it."

"You guys don't have to come."

Bess leveled her gaze at me, her hands on her hips. "Of course we're coming. We want to help."

"Yeah," George said. "Besides, I've never been to DC."

"But what about your job?" I asked, before turning to face Bess. "And Teddy?"

"Please," George scoffed. "I've worked so many double shifts and covered so many times the past few months, they owe me."

"And I've known Teddy for a few weeks," Bess added. "I've known your dad practically my entire life."

As I met my friends' eyes, I found myself at a loss for words. I wanted to tell them what their support meant to me, but I couldn't get the words to form on my tongue. There was a faint ringing in my ears and my head felt like it was encased in a thin layer of gauze, like the world wasn't quite right, and it wouldn't be again until I figured out what had happened to my dad.

There was only one way to fix this. I pointed to the computer. "Book the flight, George. We're going to DC."

The next few hours passed in a blur. George and Bess called their parents to explain what was going on and promised to check in regularly once we got to Washington. Meanwhile, I ran to my room and threw some clothes into a backpack. Then we raced to the airport, sprinting through the terminal. The flight attendant gave us a disapproving look when we slipped onto the plane just as the door was closing, panting as we collapsed into our seats.

The flight was torture. It felt like I was wasting time sitting there while Dad was missing halfway across the country. George zonked out right away and Bess immediately lost herself in a magazine someone left behind in the seat pocket, but I couldn't concentrate on the in-flight movie she'd suggested I watch to distract myself. All that was left to do was wait as the plane hurtled through the air.

After what felt like days, but was really only a

few hours, we touched down at Washington's Dulles International Airport just after noon. Bess, George, and I ran through the airport and threw ourselves into the back of the first available taxi. When we reached the city, I stared out the window at the statues of national heroes and signs pointing toward landmarks and government buildings. As we turned the corner, the Capitol Building with its distinctive dome came into view.

"I can't believe the members of Congress are in there right now making new laws," I said.

George shook her head. "I know. I've seen that building on the news and in so many movies. It's surreal to actually see it in person and to remember that people work there."

Bess nodded.

Finally we pulled up in front of the Adams Hotel. As I stepped out onto the curb, a middle-aged Asian American man sporting a pink bow tie walked through the hotel doors. He stopped suddenly as his eyes met mine.

"Nancy?"

"Yes. Are you Mr. Wei?"

"Yeah. What great timing. I stepped outside to get some air. You can spend all day in windowless rooms at these conferences and never see the sun if you're not careful. Anyway, I hope I didn't freak you out just now. I recognized you from the photo on the lock screen of your dad's phone."

"I know that photo. I'm surprised you made the connection." Dad and I had taken the selfie when we hiked to the top of Mount Erskine on Salt Spring Island, in British Columbia. We were both sweaty and I was wearing an old baseball cap.

"Well, there also aren't a lot of teenagers showing up at a hotel booked up for a lawyers' conference."

I laughed and then introduced George and Bess before we all headed into the hotel.

The lobby was gorgeous. Beams of deep mahogany crisscrossed the ceiling, and maroon-upholstered chairs and couches and potted plants were everywhere. The room was spacious, but also felt cozy. I wondered whether senators had ever met in the hotel bar to cut backroom deals the night before a crucial vote or if reporters got key sources to go on the record in those armchairs to snag their next big stories.

"So, how do you want to start?" Mr. Wei asked, jarring me from my thoughts.

"Can you walk me through the last time you saw my dad?"

"Sure. Follow me."

He led us toward the back of the hotel. Lots of people were milling around wearing business attire, badges hanging around their necks. It seemed weird at first that the conference was still in progress—that it hadn't stopped when it was discovered that Dad was missing. He should have been there chatting with other lawyers from around the country, comparing notes on recent Supreme Court decisions or the consequences of bills being debated in Congress.

And then suddenly, as if I had willed him into existence, I saw him. He was heading for the elevators to our right, away from us.

"Dad!" I cried. He didn't stop. "Dad!" I called

louder. People turned to look at me with curious looks, but my dad kept walking.

I rushed over, pushing through the conference goers, weaving past potted plants and overstuffed couches. George and Bess were right behind me, Mr. Wei trailing a little farther back.

I heard the elevator ding. I'd have only a few seconds to stop him. I darted ahead and reached out to grab him by the shoulder.

"Dad!"

He turned his head, and my stomach dropped. It wasn't my dad. The man's brow was higher, and his eyes were deeper set.

"Whoa," George said next to me, sounding as surprised as I was.

"Sorry," I gasped. "I thought you were someone else."

"Carson Drew, by any chance?" the man asked.

I nodded. "How did you know?"

"People have been mixing up the two of us the entire conference. Someone even asked if Carson and I are twins. We must be doppelgängers."

"Doppelgängers?" Bess asked.

"It's German," George explained. "It means someone who looks exactly like you, but isn't related."

The man nodded and stuck out his hand. "Chad Ford."

"Nancy Drew," I said. "I'm Carson Drew's daughter. Have you seen my dad recently?"

"No, not since yesterday."

"Okay. Sorry to have accosted you."

"No worries. I'm starting to get used to it." Mr. Ford pushed the elevator button again, and Mr. Wei shepherded us toward the back of the lobby.

"Here, most of the conference programming is being held back this way."

I stared down at my feet as we followed him, the adrenaline draining from my body. For a moment, I'd really thought it was my dad, and in those fleeting seconds, I'd been so excited and relieved.

Usually, I like solving cases. Even when they're stressful, it's fun to follow clues, and it's such a rush when the pieces come together. But this case wasn't feeling fun. I just wanted it to be over.

Bess put her hand on my shoulder. "Are you okay, Nancy? That must have been a shock."

"He really did look *a lot* like your dad," George said.

"Since when has a case been that easy to solve?" I answered with a sad smile.

We followed Mr. Wei around a corner, through a doorway, and down a long hallway.

"This is where us lawyers have been having all our fun," he said with a chuckle.

Though still nice, this part of the hotel felt newer and more industrial. The lighting turned fluorescent as gray carpeting led past walls covered in cream-striped wallpaper, broken up by a series of doors. I could hear speakers arguing passionately just beyond them.

"These are the rooms where the panels and breakout sessions are being held. The last time I saw your dad, though, we were in the grand ballroom. It shouldn't be in use now, so I can show you."

Mr. Wei led us to the end of the hallway, and we

followed him into a huge room. Rows of folding chairs filled the space, and a lectern with a microphone was set up at the front. Mr. Wei walked to the fifth row and pointed to the seat on the aisle.

"I was sitting here. I'd saved the seat next to me for your dad, but the panel he was coming from ran long, so he slipped in late. I saw him standing in the back, but when I went to check in with him after the session, which ended around eight, I couldn't find him. I didn't really think anything of it at the time. I'd just wanted to confirm our breakfast plans and figured he'd gone to have dinner with some other folks."

The room had been cleaned since the night before. I could see the lines from the vacuum in the carpet. I glanced up at the ceiling. No cameras—at least none that I could spot. It didn't appear that I was going to get anything from the room.

"Did you notice him talking to anyone?" I asked.

"I did, actually!" Mr. Wei said. "There was a woman standing next to him in the back. They were chatting when I turned around."

"And what did she look like?" I asked as I took out my notebook.

"I didn't get a great view of her. She was maybe in her forties. Average height. Brown hair pulled into a tight ponytail." He paused. I could tell that there was something else he wasn't saying.

"Was there something else?" I asked.

"Well, this is going to sound weird, but the thing I noticed most about her was that she had really good posture. Her shoulders were completely straight. Lawyers . . . we spend a lot of time hunched over our computers. Our posture is usually terrible, but hers was excellent. I found it striking."

I wrote down *good posture*, then took one more glance around the room. If there had been any clues, they'd been cleaned away the night before.

I turned to Bess and George. "I need to get into my dad's hotel room. Maybe there's something useful there."

As we headed back out to the lobby, Mr. Wei ran into someone he knew. But before we parted ways, he told me to call him if I needed anything else.

I eyed the front desk. How was I going to get a key to my dad's room?

"What are you thinking, Nance?" Bess asked. "What's the angle this time? Are you going to be an undercover starlet? A location scout for a fashion magazine? Or you could go more low-key and try to pass yourself off as a building code inspector."

I studied the woman behind the counter. She looked gruff and all business. "I think this time I'll go with the truth." George and Bess gave me skeptical looks. "Well, a variation on the truth."

I rolled the sleeves of my sweater down so they hung over my hands, then curved my shoulders and widened my eyes.

George shook her head. "It's so weird how you can do that! You look at least five years younger!"

I grinned. "That's the idea," I said before slipping into line behind a woman with a sleek bob and well-tailored business suit, while George and Bess hung back and watched.

"How can I help you, sweetie?" the receptionist

asked as I approached the counter. Her name tag said
BERTHA.

"Oh, hi," I said, raising my voice to sound young and uncertain. "I'm meeting my dad here for the weekend. He's at this conference, but then we're going to explore the capital. He's on a panel right now, but he told me to come to the front desk and get a key for his room. Carson Drew."

"All right. What's the room number?"

I arched my eyebrows up high onto my forehead, as if I was terrified. "I'm not sure. He forgot to tell me. I can text him, but I don't know if he's going to answer."

"Go ahead and try, sweetheart. I need the room number to give you a key. It's company policy."

"Okay." I pretended to text my dad but sent a message to Mr. Wei instead. Luckily, he answered right away. Room 1227. I promptly relayed the information to Bertha.

She tapped a few keys, and then a crease formed between her eyebrows. Something wasn't right.

"What? What is it?"

"Carson Drew checked out last night. . . ."

CHAPTER THREE

The Bermuda Trick

"CHECKED OUT?" I REPEATED BACK.

"Mm-hmm," she said. "Last night around eight thirty. It's an odd time, since he was charged for the night, but his room's empty, honey."

"Thanks," I said, stepping away. My mind was spinning.

I rejoined George and Bess, lost in thought. Why would Dad check out of the hotel? Mr. Wei had said the plenary ended around eight o'clock. The missed calls had started coming in at 8:23 p.m. And then my dad checked out around eight thirty, so a timeline was coming into focus. What had happened at the plenary?

"Housekeeping probably already cleaned the room, but they sometimes miss spots," I explained when I updated Bess and George about this latest twist a few minutes later. "I know the odds are long, but we need to get into that room."

"But how?" asked Bess.

I thought for a moment. "Do you guys remember what we did on that case in Bermuda when we needed to get into the tennis director's office at the resort?"

Bess's eye sparkled. "How could we forget?"

"Are you thinking we should try the same move now?" George asked.

I nodded. "You remember what to do."

"Of course!" George grinned.

We got on the elevator and pushed the button for the twelfth floor. As we were traveling up, I practiced a quick hand motion with my right hand. It had been a while since I had the maneuver down, and I hoped my skills were still up to snuff.

When the doors opened, I peered to the left,

relieved when I spotted a cart piled with towels and cleaning supplies sitting about halfway down the hall. "Phew. This will never work without housekeeping."

"Finally, some luck," George remarked.

The housekeeper was still in the room a couple of doors down from our target. I looked both ways, making sure no one else was in the hallway, before I waved, and the three of us scurried to the alcove that housed the ice machine.

After a moment, the housekeeper came out of the room, closing the door behind her, and pushed the cart to the next room away from our target. I exchanged a look with George and Bess, then nodded. It was go time.

We strode from the alcove and crossed the hallway shoulder to shoulder. I was on the far right, the same side as the cart, George took the middle, and Bess kept to the left as we hurried toward the housekeeper.

"I can't believe you forgot the tickets! We're never going to make it back before they start," I snapped, glaring at George.

"I already said I was sorry!" she spat back. "Maybe if I didn't have to keep track of *everything* on this trip and you two pitched in once in a while, I would have seen them on the desk and remembered to grab them."

"That's not fair," Bess whined. "No one asked you to plan everything. You barrel ahead without ever consulting us, and now you're blaming us for messing up. This happens on every trip, Jane, and I'm sick of it."

"Me too," I said, purposely stumbling into the housekeeper as we passed, making sure that I bumped into her hard enough that she'd have to take a step back. With my right hand, I swiped the key card clipped to her uniform with a rubber lanyard. Most housekeepers carry a master key that opens every room in the hotel. I assumed this hotel was no different.

"I am so sorry!" I exclaimed as I slipped the key into my pocket.

The woman looked surprised, and maybe a little annoyed, but said nothing.

"Watch where you're going!" George scolded me.

"It's okay," the housekeeper said, smoothing her hair back into place.

We hurried past her, making a beeline for room 1227 at the end of the hall. I swiped the key against the door's electronic pad. The light blinked red and the door remained locked despite my jostling. I swiped again. Still red. I snuck a glance down the hall, spotting the housekeeper gathering the sheets and towels she'd need for the next room. Any second now, she'd try to open the door and realize her key was missing, and then she'd be onto us.

"Hurry, Nancy," Bess whispered.

Taking a deep breath, I swiped the key against the pad one more time, holding it against the pad longer, willing my hands to stay steady. The light turned green, and releasing my breath, I pressed down on the handle and pushed the door open.

After we slinked into the room, I tossed the key onto the floor of the hallway so it would look as if it had fallen off the housekeeper's uniform.

Once the door was firmly closed, I flipped the

deadbolt so no one else could come in unexpectedly, then turned to face the room.

Bess, George, and I exchanged glances, then started to giggle. There was always a rush when you pulled off a stunt like that.

"That's such a classic move," George said, clapping her hands.

"Yeah," Bess added. "It's an oldie, but a goodie."

I was about to join in—it had been fun—when it hit me again: my dad was missing. The smile fell from my face.

Bess noticed immediately. "Let's start looking for a clue," she gently suggested.

I nodded, setting my jaw. "We need to search every nook and cranny. Housekeeping would have picked up anything obvious."

We scoured the room high and low. George crawled under the bed, using her phone as a flashlight, while Bess and I moved the dresser to see if anything had been stashed behind it. We opened all the drawers, and I even examined every page of the complimentary notepad to see if I could spot an impression left behind from a note Dad wrote before tearing away a sheet.

There was nothing.

Bess, George, and I slumped on the bed, defeated. We were sweaty and out of breath from the search, and no closer to finding any answers.

"We could check the hotel's lost and found," Bess suggested. "Maybe housekeeping did find something and left it there."

"We could," I said, half-heartedly. It felt like we were flailing around, hoping to stumble on a clue, rather than working off anything concrete. I sat up a little straighter. "Let's review what we know."

"I'll take notes," George offered. She pulled her laptop out of her backpack and got set up. "Okay, I'm ready. Shoot."

"My dad went to the plenary," I said as George tapped away. "He was late, because his previous panel ran over."

"We should confirm that," Bess interjected. "Mr.

Wei might have just been assuming that. Maybe something happened at that panel."

"Good point," I said. "At the plenary, Dad was talking to a woman with a ponytail."

"And good posture!" George added.

"Not long after the plenary ended, he called me a bunch of times. In his voice mail, I thought I heard a woman with him. And it sounded like she was taking him somewhere he didn't want to go."

"I'm really sorry about that," George said quietly. "If I wasn't so addicted to my phone, you wouldn't have locked our phones up, and you would have been able to answer, and we wouldn't be in this mess." She looked down and I could see tears rolling down her cheek. George prided herself on not crying, so I knew she was really feeling awful.

I put my hand on her shoulder. "George, the only person to blame is the person who took him. No one else."

She nodded, but I could tell she was still beating herself up about it. "Keep going. I don't want to derail us," George said, wiping her eyes.

I glanced at Bess. She always knew how to make someone feel better and was good at sensing when what they were saying wasn't the same as what they really meant. She gave me a small nod, urging me to continue.

"At eight thirty, Dad checked out of the hotel." I was quiet for a minute. "I think we need to figure out who that woman he was talking to was. She seems key to this entire situation. Unfortunately, there didn't appear to be cameras in the ballroom."

"I saw cameras in the lobby," George said. "If this mystery woman was with your dad when he checked out, we might be able to see her."

"Okay." I rose from the bed and started to pace. "We need to figure out where the security room is, get in, and hopefully find the footage from last night."

"Hold on," George said. "I might have a better idea." She got up and left the room. A few minutes later, there was a knock.

When Bess swung the door open, George was standing there, her fist still outstretched.

"Were you knocking 'America the Beautiful'?" Bess asked, eyebrow raised.

"I wanted you to know it was me. . . . And I was feeling patriotic, being in the capital and all." George turned to me. "Good news. I think we can access the cameras from right here." She pulled up a photo on her phone and zoomed in. "A lot of security cameras these days come with an app so that you can access the footage remotely. I took a photo of the cameras in the lobby and was able to make out the brand name. A magical invention called Google told me that this camera does indeed have a remote log-in option. We just need the username and password and we're all set."

"Really?"

"Yep." She handed me her phone. "Okay, Nancy, you're up first. You're going to call the front desk and get transferred to the security office. Your goal is to get the name of the supervisor."

I nodded, mentally running through a few roles that I'd used in the past when I needed to get information. Angry wife. Scared daughter. Entitled heiress.

Finally I settled on the perfect persona.

"Can you find a sound effect of a baby crying and play it really loud when I tell you to?"

"Absolutely," George said. "Just signal when."

I dialed the front desk and asked to be transferred to security. A grumpy man answered.

"Hi," I whispered. "I need to speak with your supervisor immediately."

"What? I can't hear you. Speak up."

"Sorry," I said, still talking quietly. "My baby's asleep and I'm trying not to wake him. I need to talk to your supervisor."

"Well, he's not in. It's Saturday."

"Oh, is it?" I asked with a chuckle. "When your baby only sleeps two hours—three on a good night— you lose all track of time. Can you give me his name so I can call back on Monday?"

"Can you tell me a little more about what this is regarding?" the man asked.

"There was an incident, and my boss needs to talk to him."

"Who's your boss?"

"I'm not at liberty to say, but she is a *very* important person in government." I pointed at George. She hit a button and suddenly the sound of a baby screaming their lungs out filled the room. I motioned for her to turn the volume up, almost regretting it a moment later, wincing as I resumed the con. "Oh no," I moaned over the computer-generated screams. "The baby woke up. I need to go, or he'll wake the whole building. Can you please just give me the name? My boss is not someone you want to let down. . . ."

I put the phone closer to George's computer so the screaming would blast through the phone.

"Your baby is really loud," the man shouted.

"I know. He's really upset. Can you please just give me your supervisor's name? If my boss doesn't have it in her hands in the next five minutes, I'm going to be fired, and I really need this job. Please." I wouldn't have believed it possible, but George turned the volume up even louder.

"All right. All right. His name is Doug Carr. Go take care of that baby."

As I hung up, George turned to Bess. "Okay, cuz. In five minutes, you're up."

Bess clapped, her eyes sparkling. "I assume I'm playing Doug Carr's wife? Let's hope he has one—or that the security officer doesn't know his boss very well."

George nodded. "You need to get the username and password."

Bess paced around the room, getting herself into character. If my performance had been convincing, I knew Bess's would be Oscar-worthy.

"Let's do this," she said a moment later, pulling her phone out of her bag.

She dialed the front desk and got patched through to the security room. After a ring, the same gruff man answered. Bess put on her sweetest voice. "Hi. And who do I have the pleasure of speaking with this afternoon?"

"Uh, this is Jon."

"Oh, hi, Jon. I'm glad it's you. Doug speaks so highly of you."

"He does?" Jon sounded surprised. "I always thought he didn't like me."

Bess's eyes widened, but I saw her steady herself. "Oh, you know. That's just Doug. Don't take it personally. This is his wife, by the way."

"How can I help you, Mrs. Carr?" Jon asked, a new pep in his voice.

"Well, Doug is sick as a dog and has laryngitis, so he can't speak, but there was an incident with a senator this week. She claims her watch was stolen when she was having lunch at the hotel. Doug's insisting on reviewing the footage right away, even though he should be resting. He thinks she's going to call on Monday, and he wants to be ready."

Jon gulped on the other end of the line. "I think the senator's aide just called."

Bess grinned and gave me a thumbs-up. Our two-pronged approach was working!

"Well, it's good that I called then. The thing is,

with his fever, Doug's completely spaced out on the username and password to access the security files remotely. Can you help him out?"

"Uh . . . I don't know. . . ."

Suddenly the sound of a man coughing came from the computer. Bess leaned over so Jon would hear it better. I looked over at George, beaming. That was some quick thinking.

"I know Doug would really appreciate it. Between us, he can be such a baby when he's sick. I know he'll never rest and get himself better with this little problem hanging over his head."

"All right, Mrs. Carr. The username is 'LHSecurity' and the password is 'passw0rd.' The *o* is a zero."

"Really?" Bess said, so surprised she almost dropped character.

"It's so obvious, no one would ever guess it," Jon explained.

"Well, thank you so much, Jon. Doug will never forget how you helped him out." Bess had barely hung up before George was logged into the site.

And with a few clicks, we had access to all the hotel's cameras—there were close to thirty of them. One on each hall, one in each elevator, and several covering different angles of the lobby.

"Just let me figure out how to pull up yesterday's footage. . . ." George clicked around. "Got it! Okay, I'm going to start in the elevators around eight twenty, about ten minutes before your dad checked out."

George played the footage at double speed. We watched lots of middle-aged people with badges racing up and down in the elevators, and then there he was. George slowed the speed back to normal and hit play again. Dad was in an elevator headed down, carrying his luggage. If you didn't know him, you might think he looked calm, but I could see that his eyes were a little wider than usual and his shoulders were a little closer to his ears. He was scared.

A woman stood next to him. Her hair was pulled back in a tight ponytail, she wore a black business suit, and Mr. Wei was right—her posture was amazing, shoulders and back ramrod straight. She kept her hand in her jacket pocket, but the angle seemed odd.

"George, can you zoom in?"

"Let me see." George clicked a few times and suddenly the image was bigger.

I looked more closely at the woman's pocket, and then pulled back fast.

"Oh my gosh! She has a gun!"

CHAPTER FOUR

~

Dead Zones

THERE WAS A ROARING IN MY EARS, AS IF waves were pounding inside my skull. My vision tunneled, black pushing in on all sides.

"Nancy! Are you okay? Nancy!" I could hear my friends calling to me, but they sounded a million miles away.

I was going to faint. I knew it. And then I remembered what to do. Dad had taught me on a hike in Albuquerque when I had heat exhaustion. I put my head between my knees, allowing the blood to return.

A few moments later, I felt better. My vision cleared and the roaring in my ears faded.

When I slowly lifted my head, Bess was standing in front of me, holding a glass of water.

"Thanks," I said, trying not to go red. I knew my friends weren't judging me, but I still felt pretty embarrassed.

As usual, Bess knew exactly what was going through my head. "It's okay to be scared, Nancy."

"Yeah." George put a hand on my shoulder. "What's happening is really scary."

"If you try to fight those emotions, they'll just come back even stronger," said Bess.

"I usually think Bess is a little mushy with all her feelings talk," George said with a nod, "but she's right about this."

"I know. Dad needs me, though, and I can't let my feelings get in the way."

"Look," Bess said, shifting a little closer. "Being brave isn't about not being scared. It's about doing what you need to do even when you *are* scared."

"You're right." I closed my eyes and took a deep breath. "Hit play. I can do this." I downed the rest of the water and set the glass on the bedside table with a definitive *thunk*.

George restarted the footage, and we watched my dad and the woman ride down the elevator. It felt like it took forever. My heart was racing, and I carefully avoided looking at the outline of the gun in her pocket. We didn't have time for me to freak out again.

The elevator door opened, and my dad and the woman exited and approached the reception desk, where my dad presumably checked out. When he was finished, they both turned from the desk and took a few steps, leaving the frame of the screen labeled CAMERA 3. I looked at camera four, where I assumed they would show up next, but they weren't there. I scanned the rest of the windows covering the lobby, but I didn't see my dad or the mysterious woman on any of them. "Where'd they go?"

George looked equally confused. "Hang on," she said. "We must have missed them. I'll rewind."

We watched again as Dad and the woman turned, took a few steps away from the reception desk, and then, again, disappeared.

"What's going on?" Bess asked.

Frowning, George clicked a few times, tapped out something on the keyboard, then dragged around the image on the screen. "There must be a dead zone in the lobby. A place that none of the cameras cover. I'm sure they'll pop up in a few seconds."

We watched, scanning the camera feeds. We saw Mr. Wei and another man walk through the lobby. We saw Chad Ford talking to a woman near the water cooler. We saw tons of lawyers with badges coming in and out of the lobby, but none of them were my dad or the woman.

"Where are they? They can't have disappeared," said Bess.

I thought about what George had said. "What if there was more than one dead zone, and our mystery woman knew how to navigate them so she could move through the hotel undetected?"

George bobbed her head. "That's definitely possible."

But Bess wasn't as convinced. "To plot that out would take a lot of work."

I nodded. "It would mean this was planned. That this woman came to this hotel specifically to kidnap my dad."

"I don't see another explanation," George said, meeting my eyes.

Bess put her arm around my shoulder. "I'm so sorry, Nancy."

I set my jaw. "Well, the good news is that we can do that work too. We can map the dead zones and figure out where they went." I grabbed my bag and headed toward the door. "I'm going downstairs. You two watch the monitors and direct me."

"Got it," George and Bess said in unison.

A few minutes later I was in the lobby, phone pressed to my ear. "Okay, I think I'm in the last place I saw my dad." My voice echoed, so I knew Bess had put me on speaker.

"Yep," I heard her say. "We have you in the frame."

"Okay. Let me know when you see me on a camera, and I'll reset and try again until I hit a dead zone."

"Roger that," George said.

I took two steps to my left.

"Nope, I see you on camera six," Bess chirped.

I went back to where I'd started, and then took three steps to my right.

"That's it! I can't see you," George exclaimed.

I smiled. We were making progress. "I'm going to keep going," I said, taking two more steps right.

"No! Camera eight," George cried.

I returned to my last position. "Am I off-camera again?"

"Yep, you're gone," Bess said.

"Okay, I'm going to try going forward this time." I took two steps ahead.

"Still gone!" George was getting increasingly excited.

We continued the tedious process: I walked, Bess and George monitored the cameras. Even though finding the right path was slow going, I liked having something to focus on. Finally, after forty-five minutes, I found myself standing in front of a door marked EMPLOYEES ONLY.

"Guys, I know where they went."

"Nice work, Nancy!" Bess said. "We'll be right there."

I could hear George closing her laptop and decided to settle in an overstuffed chair a few feet away while I waited for them.

A few minutes later I saw my friends rushing across the lobby and waved them over.

"So what's the plan?" George asked, her eyes gleaming. "How are we getting in there?"

I gave her a crafty smile. "Follow me."

I strode confidently back to the door, casting a quick glance over my shoulder. Thankfully, the hotel staff appeared preoccupied with the conference attendees. Palming my library card, which I'd retrieved from my bag while I'd been waiting, I slid it between the door and the frame, jostling it a few times before I heard the telltale click of the lock giving way. Without hesitating, I swung the door open and ushered Bess and George through before following, gently closing it behind me.

"I didn't have a timer going," George said, grinning, "but I think that was your fastest time yet!"

"Thanks," I said. "I've been practicing."

Bess, on the other hand, seemed a bit disappointed. "I was sure you'd have something more elaborate up your sleeve. That wasn't even a ruse."

I shrugged. "Sometimes the best con is as simple as looking like you belong. Anyway, let's see where this leads."

We were standing at the top of a stairwell. It was dark and cool. Without a word, we lit up our phones like flashlights and headed down the steps. As we descended, it became increasingly clear that this part of the hotel was never supposed to be seen by guests. The paint on the walls was chipping and the stairs creaked under our feet. While the lobby and guest rooms had felt old in a charming way, this space was just decrepit.

The staircase led down to a large basement. Stacks of old furniture and room-service carts lined the walls and crowded the floor.

"EEEK!" Bess screeched. Startled, George grabbed my arm, her nails digging into my skin. "What? What is it?"

Bess didn't answer. I followed her gaze to a ghostly figure looming over us. An eerie moaning sound wafted through the basement, and we quickly grabbed hands.

"It's coming our way," George hissed.

I nodded, but then I looked closer. "It's moving, but I'm not sure it's moving toward us." I took a step forward and cautiously reached out my hand, steeling myself. As soon as my fingers brushed our "phantom," I couldn't help letting out a chuckle. "It's not a ghost! It's just a sheet draped over discarded furniture. Here, watch."

I yanked on the fabric, revealing a coat stand sitting on top of a desk.

"Sorry," Bess said sheepishly. "I don't know why I freaked out."

"It's okay," I said, giving her a reassuring smile. "We're all on edge, and it did look pretty scary."

"I still hear moaning," George whispered.

I paused, listening. "It sounds like it's coming from that direction." I pointed toward the far side of the room.

Bess learned forward. "I think I see light coming from there too."

"It's probably a door." I took a determined step toward the corner. "I bet that's how the woman took my dad out of the hotel."

Maneuvering through the stacks of discarded furniture, Bess, George, and I picked a path through the clutter. Some of the piles nearly brushed the ceiling. They creaked and swayed as we shimmied past.

"This is like a furniture graveyard," George muttered.

"I was thinking it was like a furniture version of those hedge mazes you find in fancy gardens," I said as my hand brushed a chair with only three legs.

"Do you think they redecorated the rooms but kept

all the old stuff, just in case they changed their minds?" Bess asked, wrinkling her nose.

Before I could respond, there was a clatter behind us. George yelped.

"What was that?" I demanded, my eyes darting around the room.

"Nothing," George said. "Just hit my shin on what I think might have once been a luggage rack."

My foot made contact with something, sending it skittering across the floor. The beam of my camera light caught the object just as it slid under a narrow gap beneath a dresser piled high with TVs and ottomans.

"I think that was a phone!" I said. "What if it's my dad's?"

"That's a big leap, Nancy," George said. "It could have been anything. An even if it *is* a phone, it's way more likely to belong to one of the hotel employees. And that very tall pile of very heavy furniture looks like it might topple over at the smallest nudge," she added, grabbing my elbow as I made to rush over to the dresser for a closer look.

"The Find My Phone app said Dad's phone was in the hotel, even after he went missing. This could explain it," I insisted.

George took a breath, about to answer, but Bess interrupted before she could say anything. "George, what's gotten into you? You know if there's any chance that the object could be Mr. Drew's phone, we have to check."

"You're right. I'm sorry." George shuddered. "This basement just creeps me out."

"Step back," I instructed, before lying down on the ground and sliding my arm under the dresser.

"Careful!" Bess warned.

Dust tickled at my nose. I held my breath, fighting as hard as I could, but the sneeze exploded out of me. An ominous groaning sounded above me as the TVs swayed. I heard Bess gasp and I clenched my eyes shut, sure that the junk pile was about to come crashing down on my back.

After a moment, the pile settled, and I let out a sigh of a relief before slowly sweeping my arm back and forth through the grime, feeling for the phone's plastic case. "I can't reach it!"

"Let me guide you," George said. She lay down at the end of the dresser and shined her phone's light at the shadows. "Okay, Nance. More to your right."

I slid my arm as directed, but I didn't feel anything.

"You're so close. Just a little more."

I stretched my arm, extending my fingers as far as they would go.

George shifted her position, sending up another cloud of dust. "A little farther . . ."

"Come on, Nancy," Bess urged. "You can do it."

The tips of my fingers brushed the plastic edge, but I couldn't get enough purchase to grab hold of it and drag it out.

Finally I pulled my arm out with a sigh. "I can't reach."

"Wait!" Bess shot to attention. "I have an idea!" She quickly but carefully wound her way back through the maze of clutter. I heard clanging mixed with unintelligible grunts and muttering.

"Bess, what are you doing?"

"Hang on!" There was more clanging, then the sound of fabric being torn. Moments later, Bess returned sweaty, her hair a mess, but she was smiling. She triumphantly held up a metal pole bent at one end. "I thought we could use this as a hook."

George sat up, squinting at the pole. "Is that the leg of a luggage rack?"

"Yep! I remembered you said you ran into one."

"Bess, you're a genius!" I said as I took the pole and slid it under the dresser.

"Let's try again," George said. "Back and to the right."

"I feel like I'm playing one of those claw games. You know, the ones where you try to grab a stuffed animal, but it always slips away just as the claw rises up again."

"Don't say that!" Bess scolded. "Those things are impossible."

I felt the pole make contact with the object. "Got it!" I called out.

Carefully, I guided the mystery object back toward me, raising it in the air as I sat up. "And guys, I'm pretty sure this is Dad's phone."

I was covered head to toe in dust, but at least I'd gotten my prize.

George and Bess crowded around me as I bent over the screen, tapping to wake up the phone. The battery was at a measly three percent.

"Do you know your dad's password?" George asked.

"Of course." I entered the numbers without even thinking. But instead of Dad's home screen, the screen filled with his notes app. NANCY: 16.

"Sixteen? What does that mean?" Bess asked.

I racked my brain, before deflating at the truth. "I have no idea."

CHAPTER FIVE

A New Twist

PHONE RECOVERED, WE TURNED OUR attention back to the door, which opened into a rear alley. Following the narrow passage, found ourselves across the street from a parklet with a bench that wrapped around a tree. I took a deep lungful of fresh air as we plopped down. It felt good to be out of that dark, dusty, overcrowded basement.

After taking in a few more deep breaths, I turned my attention back to the screen of Dad's phone. *Sixteen.* What was he trying to tell me? "It has to be some kind of riddle."

"You and your dad do love puzzles," Bess said.

It's true. Dad had me helping him solve crossword puzzles and sudoku games as soon as I could read. One year we'd even gone on vacation to a swanky resort in upstate New York that included guest talks from puzzle experts, afternoon board game tournaments, and a scavenger hunt that lasted all weekend. It had been one of my favorite trips.

"If this were a puzzle, the 'sixteen' wouldn't be literal—it would be standing in for something else. Let's brainstorm. Do you think Dad meant us to connect the sixteen to Washington, DC, in some way?" I asked. I got up from the bench and started pacing. I always think better when I pace.

"The White House is at 1600 Pennsylvania Avenue," George said.

"True," I said, not bothering to pause. "But it's pretty unlikely that she was escorting him to dinner with the president."

"There's a Sixteenth Street here in DC," Bess said, looking up from her phone. "Maybe he figured out they were going there."

"Maybe," I said, but it felt off. When you're doing a puzzle, whether it's a crossword or trying to break out of an escape room, there's a moment where everything clicks into place, and you know that you and the puzzle maker are on the same wavelength. I know how my dad's brain works. He's a precise person. He wouldn't send us on a wild-goose chase, poking around an entire street. Even in a rush, even under pressure, he would have come up with a clue that would lead me exactly where I needed to go.

"Let's keep thinking," I said. "Sixteen. *Sixteen.* You get your driver's license at sixteen. Is there a car museum in DC?"

"Let me check," George said, as she whipped out her phone. "No car museum. There is a car collection at the Museum of American History, though."

"That's a possibility." But it still didn't feel right.

"There are sixteen ounces in a pound," Bess offered.

George kept scrolling. "Abraham Lincoln was the sixteenth president."

I looked at her, eyes wide. "That's it," I squawked.

"The Lincoln Memorial. It's on the National Mall." I knew that was where Dad wanted us to go just like I know when a word will fit perfectly into the black-and-white grid of the crossword puzzle without even having to count the number of letters.

Twenty minutes later we were racing up the same steps where Martin Luther King Jr. had delivered his "I Have a Dream" speech, but I was so focused on finding my dad, I didn't really have time to take in the significance of the moment. I wasn't naive enough to think that my dad would still be at the memorial. He'd left the note on his phone almost a day ago. But I hoped that even if we didn't find Dad there, we'd find another clue.

But all the thoughts racing through my mind evaporated as I stared up at the enormous statue of President Lincoln sitting ramrod straight in his chair, staring down at the country he'd shepherded over one hundred fifty years ago. His eyes looked sad, but patient. I had seen photos of the memorial in my history textbooks, but I wasn't prepared for how big it was. Or how awe-inspiring it would be. Tourists swarmed around us, jostling for the best place to take their selfies. Small children shrieked, delighted by how their voices echoed. But as I gazed up at Lincoln's face, the pandemonium around me faded. I found myself mesmerized by the details of the statue: the way Lincoln's brow was slightly furrowed, and how his hands seemed tense and restless, even as the statue itself projected calm. I found myself a little overwhelmed and grateful that this man had overseen our country during one of its most tumultuous times.

"It's beautiful," Bess whispered next to me.

"It really is," I agreed.

When I glanced over at George, she was discreetly wiping tears from her eyes.

"Daddy! Pick me up!" a little girl demanded from a few feet away. Her outburst snapped my attention back to our task. I hadn't come to the memorial to think about the country or to admire the architecture. I was there to find my dad. "Okay. We're looking for proof my dad was here, so that we can hopefully figure out our next step."

"Any idea what we're looking for?" George asked.

I shrugged. "I really don't know. Anything that seems out of the ordinary? I'm hoping that whatever it is, I'll know it when I see it." I took in the awesome scope of the memorial again, feeling momentarily overwhelmed. "George, you search the left side. Bess, you take the middle, and I'll take the right. Text if you spot anything."

I headed to the back right corner of the building and walked along the wall, keeping my eyes trained on the ground. I could tell people around me thought I was acting a little strange, but in that moment, I didn't care. My plan was to work my section methodically, walking up and down in a grid pattern and hoping something would jump out at me.

After a few minutes, I stole a look across the way and saw that Bess and George had each had a similar idea and were walking their own grids. I smiled. I was so grateful to have them with me.

After my third turn, all I'd found were ice cream wrappers and water bottles, and I was starting to lose hope. The memorial was probably cleaned regularly, so if Dad had even left a clue, it probably would have been swept up or wiped away long before I got there. But if there was even the slightest chance of finding something, I had to keep looking.

As I squared my shoulders for another pass, out of the corner of my eye, I spotted something flashing. A gold object had been wedged into the wall opposite me in the gap where the wall met the floor. Abandoning the search plan, I rushed over, heart racing as I prodded at the spot. After a few careful pokes, the item dropped from the crack, landing in my palm. I gasped as I took in the gold tiepin I'd given Dad for his birthday—a small circle, about the size of a dime, engraved with Dad's initials.

"He was here!" I yelped louder than I meant to, my voice echoing off the marble. Everyone nearby turned to look. I felt my cheeks go pink, but I was too happy to care.

Bess and George jogged over, and I held out the tiepin.

"I'm so relieved," George said. "All I managed to spot was food wrappers. I can't believe people litter in a place like this."

Bess made a face. "It's disgusting."

"What's our next move, Nancy?" George asked.

I looked around. It was a good question. We knew my dad had been here, but then what? Where had he gone? I studied the pin, just in case Dad had left another hint, like his note on the phone, but there was nothing. My stomach sank in disappointment.

"That's it?" George asked. "I mean, I guess now we have proof that Mr. Drew was here, but it's kind of a dead end."

The way she emphasized the last sentence reminded me of lonely-looking graffiti on a park bench or overpass: *So-and-so was here.*

"Okay. So what now?" Bess asked, furrowing her brow.

We stood at the top of the memorial steps, taking in the reflecting pool that stretched toward the Washington Monument. The giant column with its triangular top was an impressive sight, rising starkly against the late afternoon sky. And farther off were other national monuments sure to be on any tourist's must-see list, including memorials honoring veterans and fallen soldiers of the Vietnam War, the Korean War, and World War II. Dad wouldn't just drop a clue in the middle of the lawn. He'd leave it at a landmark, where I would have a better chance of finding it. But there was no way to know which direction his captor had taken him or which monument to search first. I sighed. We were going to have to split up again.

Before we parted ways, Bess and George agreed to send pictures of anything unusual they found, and then I was jogging toward the Vietnam Veterans Memorial. Sweat poured down my face. It was so humid, it felt like I was swimming through the air.

I slowed as I approached the memorial, two black granite walls that started just a few inches off the ground and gradually got higher and higher until they met. It looked like a black scar sharply cutting though the bright green lawn. I didn't have the same feeling of awe I'd had at the Lincoln Memorial, but the hairs on the back of my neck were standing up, like I was about to walk into a dark room and didn't know what was waiting for me.

I walked slowly along the wall and saw that names were engraved into it. A chill passed through me as it hit me that they were all soldiers who'd died in the war. Flowers, teddy bears, and other mementos lined the base of the stone, and from my vantage point, it looked like one long grave marker. I shook my head and continued along, scanning the ground for anything Dad might have dropped, careful not to disturb anyone there paying their respects.

A stifled sob stopped me short. The wall now towered several feet above me, covered top to bottom in names. I looked ahead and saw an older woman with long gray hair standing a few feet in front of me, tears streaming down her face. She gently touched one of the names, clutching a rose in her other hand. I turned away to give her a little privacy and studied the inscriptions before me, stepping back suddenly when I caught my reflection staring at me in the polished granite. It was like I was being confronted by the names of the dead.

The woman let out another small cry. I turned toward her, and this time her eyes met mine.

"Forgive me. He was my first love. I still miss him."

"I'm so sorry." I couldn't imagine losing Ned. We spent a lot of time apart, but I always knew I'd see him in a few days or weeks, at most.

My phone buzzed. George had texted Bess and me a photo of a button followed by a string of question marks. I expanded the image for a closer look, then huffed in frustration. There was nothing special about it—it was just a plain white button. Sure, it could have come from one of Dad's dress shirts, but it could have belonged to a million other people too.

I sent back a shrugging emoji, then returned my attention to the woman, giving her a sad smile before I continued to make my way down the wall.

After searching for a few more minutes, it became increasingly apparent that I wasn't going to spot anything Dad had left. And as I stared out at the perfectly manicured lawn that stretched before the walls, it struck me that there wasn't much that he could have left. Would he have been able to take off his belt? If he dropped his watch, someone would probably have found it and carried it home. We'd been incredibly lucky to find his phone and his tie-pin, but at some point our luck would run out. We needed a new plan.

My stomach rumbled. All I'd eaten during the day was a small bag of pretzels on the plane. I was starving. George and Bess must be too.

As the sun dipped behind the trees, I texted my friends to announce I was calling the search off and to meet me back at the Lincoln Memorial.

I found them sitting on the steps, looking like they'd just run a marathon. Bess's hair, usually perfectly styled, hung limp, wet with sweat. George's cheeks were bright pink and her eyes were glassy. I didn't even want to know what I looked like.

"First things first," I declared. "We need food."

"Yes." George groaned. "I think I can feel my stomach eating itself."

"Stop being so dramatic, George!" Bess scolded. "I saw a diner a couple of blocks from our hotel on our way in from the airport. Should we try there?"

"I don't care where we go, as long as they serve big portions," George said, slumping down.

Forty-five minutes later, we were sitting in a booth enjoying high-quality air-conditioning and good old American grease. We hadn't said so much as a word to one another once our meals arrived. We were too busy shoveling food into our mouths.

"What's the plan for tomorrow?" George asked as she cut off another huge bite of pancake. She'd insisted that since it was her first meal of the day, it needed to be breakfast.

"We go back to basics," I said after wiping my mouth. "We only talked to Mr. Wei. We should interview the hotel staff. The woman from the video had to have spent some time in the hotel if she knew where the camera dead zones are. Maybe someone saw something."

"We could also talk to more of the conference attendees," Bess suggested. "Find out what happened in that panel before the plenary."

"That's a lot of people to talk to. We'll probably need to divide and conquer," George said.

It felt good to have a plan.

After we finished our meal, we headed back to the hotel. I booked us a room, and we piled onto the king-size bed, barely making it to nine before we all agreed it was time to turn in.

But even though I was exhausted, I couldn't really sleep. Every time I closed my eyes, I saw the surveillance footage from the elevator and the outline of the gun pointed at my dad. Sometime after four, I drifted off to sleep.

The next morning I was in the lobby, grabbing a third cup of coffee from the breakfast buffet while George and Bess finished getting ready in the room, when my phone rang. I didn't recognize the number, but the caller ID said it was a Baltimore area code. I wasn't exactly sure how far that was from DC, but I knew Maryland bordered the District, so it couldn't be too far.

"Hello?"

There was a pause. I could hear breathing on the other end of the line.

"Hello?" I repeated.

"Is this Nancy Drew?" a woman's voice finally said.

"Yes."

"I'm with your father."

My jaw dropped. "What? Where? Who are you?"

"I'll text you the address." And with that, she hung up. I called back immediately, but it went straight to voice mail.

A few seconds later a text message came in: 509 N. Oxford Ave., Baltimore.

I called George and Bess and quickly caught them up. A few minutes later we were in a rideshare heading to Baltimore.

It took about an hour to get there. My heart was thundering the entire time. I should have demanded that the woman prove what she was saying—and that my dad was safe. I should have asked her to send a photo, but the whole call had happened so fast.

As we drove through Baltimore, the neighborhoods changed a lot. Some were run-down with boarded-up houses and closed stores. Others had brightly painted houses and trendy cafés full of hipsters in fedoras.

The driver turned off a commercial strip onto a tree-lined street with narrow brick houses that abutted one another.

"What's the deal with these houses?" George asked the driver. My friends and I sometimes seemed to share the same brain.

"Oh, those are called row houses. Baltimore is known for them. The city grew really fast, so one builder would just build a whole block at a time."

George held up her phone and started snapping pictures. "They're so cool. These shots will look great on my Instagram."

The driver pulled over. "Okay, here you are." I'd

given him an address around the corner so that we could suss out the location.

As we got out of the car, George brought up a map on her phone. "The house should be about halfway down that block on the right."

A couple of houses away I stopped, pointing at a car parked across from the place we were looking for. "You guys should hide there, just in case. I'm going to see if I can peek through the window and get a read on the situation before I ring the doorbell. If anything goes wrong, call the police."

"I don't think you should go by yourself, Nancy," Bess said, her concern clear.

"Yeah," George agreed. "You're talking about confronting a kidnapper who we know has a gun. This isn't safe!"

"That's why I want you guys to keep a lookout and be my backup. The fewer people in danger, the better."

George and Bess exchanged a worried look.

"I trust you two to watch my back. I know I can rely on you if anything bad happens."

"Okay," Bess finally agreed. She and George crouched behind the car's bumper, and I took a deep breath before creeping up to the house. Standing on my tiptoes, I looked through a small window at the top of the front door. I could just see into the dining room. Dad was sitting at a table. He looked tired but didn't appear injured. Across from him, I saw the same woman from the security footage. Her hands were twitching, and her eyes never seemed to stay focused in one place for more than a few seconds. The gun we'd seen in her jacket pocket was now sitting in front of her on the table, and though she wasn't threatening Dad at the moment, it was still too close for comfort.

I wished there was a way I could get Dad's attention without alerting his captor.

The best way forward really did seem to be ringing the doorbell.

I took a deep breath, walked up to the front door, and pushed the small button. A moment later I heard footsteps, and then there was my dad standing in the doorway.

He broke into a huge smile. "Nancy! Thank goodness! I'm so happy to see you!"

"Dad! What's going on? Are you okay?"

He wrapped me in a big hug. As he held me against his chest, I could feel his muscles tensing. He wasn't nearly as relaxed as he was acting.

"Dad! Just tell me what's going on," I whispered.

"I'm fine. I'm fine. Don't worry," Dad said at a normal volume. He released me, and his gaze focused on a point across the street. "George! Bess! I know you're out there. Come out, come out, wherever you are."

My friends cautiously stood up from behind the car but didn't come any closer. I studied Dad's face, looking for a hint, a signal, anything, but his face was still frozen in that same wide smile. With a sigh, I waved to George and Bess.

"Come on inside," Dad said, overly cheerful as he put his hands on my shoulders. "I have a case for you."

CHAPTER SIX

An Explanation

A CASE? FINDING MY DAD WAS MY CASE. "I saw the gun," I whispered. "I'm calling the police." But when I pulled out my phone, Dad snatched it from my hand.

"I know I scared you, but everything is going to be fine now."

I couldn't help but notice his use of the word "now." Dad was always careful with the language he used. Clearly, things had not been fine earlier.

George and Bess followed us into a foyer, and then Dad led us to the dining room, where the woman was still sitting, staring off into space, the gun still lying before her ominously. She didn't appear to have moved so much as a centimeter.

"Nancy, this is Kim. Kim, this is my daughter, Nancy. Remember, I told you about her? And these are her friends, George and Bess."

Bess's eyes were wide, fixed on the gun. George's gaze met mine, and her eyebrows wrinkled in confusion. What was going on? Why was Dad acting like we were meeting an old friend of his, rather than the person who'd kidnapped him? Why hadn't he let me call the police?

Dad nudged me gently. "Remember your manners, Nancy."

"Hi," I said as brightly as I could muster.

Kim finally turned to take us in, but her expression didn't change. She looked tired—like the very act of breathing was exhausting.

"Have a seat," my dad said, pulling out a chair for me. "You too, George and Bess." He turned to Kim. "I'm going to go to the kitchen and get the girls some water. Is that okay?"

Kim nodded, and my dad quietly slipped out of the room. I looked around, taking in my surroundings. The dining room was nice, or it had been once. The table was covered in a striped tablecloth that seemed like it hadn't been changed in months. There were cobwebs in the corners, and through the doorway leading to the kitchen, I saw dishes piled in the sink. This was the house of someone who was barely holding it together. Kim seemed broken, like something terrible had happened to her.

Dad returned and handed glasses around, before cautiously turning back to Kim. "Should we fill the girls in on how I ended up in your company?"

Kim nodded, but remained silent.

After a moment, Dad cast her a sympathetic look, then cleared his throat. "Two nights ago, there was a little mix-up. Kim approached me at the plenary. . . ."

I noticed how carefully Dad emphasized *approached*. Threatening someone with a gun was a little more aggressive than the word implied. I could tell he was being careful not to upset Kim, so I decided the smart thing to do would be to follow his lead.

"You see, Kim was under the impression that I was someone else," he continued.

I looked up sharply. Now things were making a little more sense. "Did you think he was Chad Ford?" I asked, recalling the man in the hotel lobby who had looked so much like my dad.

"Oh, you met Chad?" Dad asked.

George started bouncing in her seat. "Nancy thought he was you!"

"We all did," Bess added.

Dad reached over and patted Kim on the arm. "See, I told you it was nothing to be embarrassed about." She nodded and even managed a small smile.

"Did Chad tell you what he does?" Dad asked. I shook my head. "He's a prosecutor here in Baltimore. He actually prosecuted Kim's son, Walker."

"Wrongfully!" Kim shouted.

I was so surprised to hear her speak—and at such volume—that I jumped, scraping the chair on the floor.

"My son is innocent," she said a little more quietly.

"Why don't you tell the girls what happened?" Dad calmly suggested.

Kim took a deep breath and met my eyes for the first time, sizing me up as if to measure my trustworthiness. I tried to seem open and accepting to whatever she had to say, but the truth was she made me nervous.

"Last year I was deployed to Afghanistan. I'm a Marine." That explained her perfect posture. "My son Walker is nineteen. His dad passed away three years ago, so Walker was here on his own. I thought it would be okay. He was staying in the house, working at a jewelry store in a nearby town while he was taking classes at the local community college. Everything was going great. He liked his job and the people he worked with. He was doing well in his classes. It was hard to talk while I was over there, but when we did, he sounded happy." She paused and wiped tears from her eyes. "Sorry. Anyway, one night someone stole over a million dollars' worth of diamond engagement rings from the store's safe. Before

I even knew what was happening, Walker was arrested and charged with grand theft."

"Why him?" I asked.

"He didn't have an alibi. The robbery happened around ten. Walker had come home and gone straight to sleep." She shifted and looked down, avoiding my eyes. I could tell she was holding something back.

"Kim, you have to tell them everything," Dad urged quietly.

She sighed. "Each employee had their own code to get past the store's security system. Whoever the thief was, they used Walker's code."

George, Bess, and I exchanged glances. That explained why the police had suspected him.

BAM! Kim had slammed the gun on the table and was glaring at us.

"I saw that look. You don't believe me."

I caught Dad's eye, gave him a small nod, and turned back to Kim.

"I don't know enough about the situation to have an opinion on Walker's guilt or innocence," I said soothingly. She narrowed her eyes, and I saw her hand tighten around the grip. "The security code is a compelling piece of evidence, though," I added quickly. When someone is this on edge, you can't lie to them. If you come across as patronizing or condescending, it'll just set them off. "I'd like to hear more of your side of the story. How do you know Walker didn't steal the jewelry?"

Kim remained silent. Under the table, I could feel George fidgeting. Bess, seated beside me, was taking slow, steady breaths.

Finally Kim pushed the gun away. "Okay."

I felt my shoulders relax. I hadn't realized just how high they'd risen as I tried to defuse the situation.

"Look, I'm not crazy. I understand why the police questioned Walker. Of course they should've questioned him. Even if he had an airtight alibi and his security code hadn't been used, the officers were just doing their jobs. Walker worked at the store. He might have known something that could help in their investigation. But the cops got lazy. You said the security code was compelling evidence. Sure, but if Walker wanted to rob the store, he wouldn't have used his own code. That would be stupid. And my son is not stupid."

"It's weird the police didn't think of that," George said.

"They did, but they wanted to close the case. Look the other way so they could get a win."

"The police are under a lot of pressure to close cases," Dad said. "Sometimes they take shortcuts. A prosecutor shouldn't pursue a case that clearly hasn't been investigated thoroughly, but they're also under pressure."

Kim nodded. "I was stuck overseas, and I couldn't afford to get my son a fancy lawyer. The public defender he was assigned pushed him to take the plea deal Chad was offering. The lawyer said the sentence would be lighter if Walker confessed, and with a chance that he would lose at trial, my son got scared. He agreed to plead guilty. He was over eighteen. There was nothing I could do to stop him from taking the deal."

Kim looked down and took a breath. I could feel

how frustrated and powerless she felt that she'd been unable to protect her son.

"For the past year, I've been sending letters and trying get a meeting with Chad Ford. He could help me overturn this wrongful conviction. But he's ignored me. His assistant takes my messages but never seems to pass them along. My letters and emails have gone unanswered. I even spent an entire day sitting in his office, but someone must have tipped him off that I was there, because he came and went through the back. I never even saw him."

I wondered how Kim knew that Chad was even in that day. Maybe he hadn't been avoiding her. He could have been in court or working from home. Still, she was clearly fragile, and I wasn't going to risk pointing out flaws in her logic.

"Finally, I couldn't wait anymore," Kim continued.

"What happened?" Bess asked.

"Sorry," Kim said with a sniffle, brushing away tears running down her cheeks. "Last week Walker got into a fight with someone at the correctional facility.

It was some kind of misunderstanding. I don't know the details, but he got beat up pretty bad. He'll never survive ten years in there. My boy is not cut out for prison life. I need to get him out. And I was desperate. When I was in Chad Ford's office that day, I overheard his assistant making arrangements for him to go to the conference in DC, so I went to the hotel to convince him, but . . ." She trailed off, but I didn't need her to explain the rest. Clearly, her meeting had not gone as planned, and she'd ended up with my dad instead.

"This is where you come in, Nancy." Dad looked serious but certain. I wished I felt as confident.

"Are you saying you want me to prove that Walker is innocent?"

He nodded. "We need you to find the real thief. It's the only way the state will overturn Walker's conviction."

"You'll help, right?" I asked.

My dad grimaced, and I felt my stomach sink. It looked like his arrangement with Kim was much more complicated than I'd hoped. "I promised Kim I'd stay with her."

"I don't know you," Kim said. "Your dad says I can trust you, but I'm already taking a gamble on his word that you won't call the police, and if I let him go, how do I know you won't flee back to River Heights without lifting a finger for Walker? He needs help."

"I've never walked away from a case," I said, sitting up a little straighter. "If I say I'm going to solve something, I solve it."

Kim shrugged. "I need more assurance than that."

I could have kept arguing, but I could tell from the look on her face that she wasn't going to budge.

"Can I use your restroom before I get started?" I asked.

Dad stood up. "I'll show you where it is."

"Hurry back," George urged under her breath as I passed her chair.

Dad led me down a hallway lined with family photos. Walker's childhood had been lovingly documented. There were photos of Little League games and soccer tournaments, birthday parties and family vacations, spelling bees and piano recitals. Kim looked so happy in the pictures. I would never have guessed that the woman in the snapshots was the person sitting in the dining room. In the photos, her eyes sparkled and her skin glowed. She looked healthy, not like she'd barely eaten in months.

A man—I assumed it was her husband—was in most of the images. If you looked carefully, you could see him get sicker over the years, until he just disappeared. I felt a pang of sympathy. Kim had had a lot of bad things happen to her, not to mention whatever terrible things she'd seen while deployed. She must be dealing with a lot of trauma.

"Dad," I whispered when we were far enough away from the dining room that I was confident Kim wouldn't overhear us. "Do you really want me to solve this case? Because I could call the police as soon as I leave."

He shook his head. "Don't do that. I don't want Kim to get in trouble."

"Dad, she kidnapped you."

"She made a bad choice, sure, but the pain

motivating her is real. And from all she's told me, I think she might be right about her son. I don't think the police investigated properly. Chad Ford should have refused to prosecute on such flimsy evidence, and Walker's lawyer bullied him into taking a bad plea deal. He shouldn't have to stay in prison for a crime he didn't commit because his mom made a mistake."

"Okay. It makes me really nervous to leave you here with her, though."

Dad put his hands on my shoulders. "I've dealt with some tough characters. I can take care of myself. Right now, I need you focused on what you do best: solving a mystery."

"It's going to be hard. The crime happened over a year ago. If there were clues, most of them are probably gone."

Dad stared right into my eyes. "I know this is hard. And scary. You're worried about my safety. I'm asking a lot of you. But I wouldn't ask it if I didn't know you'd succeed. You're an amazing detective, and you can do this."

I nodded, even though I felt like I was going to cry. "What if after I investigate, I find out that Walker really did steal the diamond rings?"

"We'll cross that bridge when we come to it. For now, treat this like any of your other cases."

"I'll try." I gave Dad a tight hug. "Oh." I said after a moment, pulling back and reaching into my purse. "I thought you might want these back."

Dad's face lit up with the first genuine smile I'd seen since he'd opened Kim's door as I handed him his tiepin and phone. "You found them! I hated leaving these behind, especially the pin. You know how much it means to me. But it was the best I could come up with in the moment."

"How'd you manage to drop them without Kim noticing? And how'd you call me so many times? I'm surprised she didn't take your phone."

"Well, you're not the only crafty one in the family, Nancy. But there was some luck involved too. As Kim was escorting me out of the plenary, I think she was going to demand I give her my phone when a woman approached us and asked for a restaurant recommendation for dinner.

Kim got frazzled and must have forgotten about my phone. You have to remember, she did all this as a last resort. She's not used to breaking the law. She was stressed, and that made her distracted. I'd put in a quick call to the office after my last panel—I was late to the plenary as a result— so the phone app was open, and you know you're the top of my favorites list. So with the phone in my pocket, I kept hitting your number.

When we were in the basement, Kim stumbled, and as she was collecting herself, I managed to get the Notes app open. I knew I didn't have much time, so I couldn't type a long message. Kim had told me we'd be paying a visit to Lincoln, and I just hoped you'd figure out what sixteen meant. Of course you, my clever detecting daughter, did just that. Later, inspired by Kim's tumble, I faked tripping to drop the phone. Some well-timed coughs covered the tiepin and the cuff links."

"Cuff links? Sorry. I guess we missed them."

Dad grabbed my hand and squeezed it. "You did an amazing job finding what you did. I knew the odds were long. And they weren't great clues, anyway. I was improvising. I wanted you to know where I'd been, even though I didn't know how many places she'd take me."

Something occurred to me then. "Why did she even take you to the National Mall? It seems a strange detour during a kidnapping."

"She was trying to appeal to my sense of American values of justice—or Chad's, since at that point she still didn't believe that I wasn't him. She thought it would help her argument that he was innocent and help convince me to overturn Walker's conviction."

"I guess I should get started."

Dad gave my hand another squeeze, then headed back to the dining room, while I went into the bathroom and splashed water on my face. It wasn't even noon, and it had already been a long day. At least I knew Dad was safe, though I'd feel a lot better when he was far away from Kim.

When I walked back into the dining room, everyone was sitting around the table in awkward silence.

"Okay," I said looking at George, Bess, and then finally my dad. "Let's go solve a diamond heist."

CHAPTER SEVEN

On the Inside

KIM TOLD US THE NAME OF THE STORE where Walker had worked and explained the process for requesting a visit with him at the correctional facility.

When I gave my dad one last tight hug, I didn't want to let him go. It felt wrong to leave him with Kim. Still, I trusted him when he said this was the best path forward.

"Go get 'em," he murmured into my hair.

As soon as the door closed behind us, George sighed dramatically. "That was intense!"

I held my finger to my lips, then pointed down

the block. I didn't know how much Kim could hear through the door, and I didn't want to do anything that would get her more upset.

George nodded. As soon as we rounded the corner, I collapsed under a tree. I didn't care if it looked weird. The adrenaline that had kept me focused inside the house was draining out of me, and I suddenly felt exhausted.

As George and Bess flopped next to me, I noticed that George's collar was drenched with sweat. Bess's cheeks had gone a chalky white. They must have felt as terrified as I did.

"I'm sorry, George. I wasn't trying to be rude."

"I get it. I shouldn't have said anything. It just kind of blurted out."

"That whole thing was intense," I said. "Kim is intense."

"She's been through a lot," said Bess. I loved that she could always find the good in someone, even if they'd done something awful.

"The best thing we can do for Kim and my dad is

to find those stolen diamonds as quickly as possible. While I'm meeting with Walker at the correctional facility, can you guys head to the jewelry store and do some preliminary poking around?"

"We're on it," chirped Bess. "Don't worry, Nancy. We'll crack this."

"I know we will. But with a case this cold, it could take weeks, and we don't have that kind of time. I want my dad out of that house as soon as possible."

A car pulled up to the curb. "That's your ride," George said.

"You already called a car?"

"Time is of the essence, right? I'm not a crackerjack detective like you, but at least I can make sure you don't have to wait for a ride." She grinned.

"You two are the best! Thank you for everything."

"We'll see you soon," Bess said.

Half an hour later, my car pulled up outside a large brick building that had barbed wire lining the tops of the walls. For some reason, I'd always thought prisons were in small towns, keeping inmates removed from the rest of the population, but this facility was right in downtown Baltimore. We'd passed signs for an art museum and city hall on the way.

"Are you sure this is the right address?" the driver asked.

"Yep, this is it."

The driver raised his eyebrows but remained silent.

After getting out, I took a deep breath and walked toward the guard station. I've solved a lot of cases, and I know that people break the law for all sorts of reasons. Most of them are good folks who got themselves in bad situations and made a poor decision.

Even though I knew there was no reason to be worried, I still felt jittery. As I approached the desk, the guard looked me up and down. I could tell he was wondering what I was doing there, but he didn't ask any questions. "ID, please."

I handed over my driver's license.

"From out of town, huh?" I nodded. The guard typed my name into the computer. "You're here to see

Walker Johnson?" I nodded again. Kim had said she'd call ahead and put my name on the list. I was glad she'd managed to do it. "All right, young lady. Come on through."

The door buzzed loudly, and I stepped past the sensor, which beeped loudly. I look over at the guard, who sighed wearily. "Wait there," he said, grudgingly rising from his chair.

As he made his way to me, I took in a utilitarian hallway lit with bright fluorescents. One of the bulbs was on the fritz, blinking and buzzing loudly. The combination made my head throb. The floors were clean, but grungy. I couldn't imagine how the guards worked there all day.

The guard approached with a wand and waved it over me.

"You can't bring that in with you," he said, pointing at my bag.

"What should I do with it?"

He pointed at a bank of lockers across the way. "You can stow it in there."

I crossed over to secure my bag. The lockers were small and dented, and many were filled with trash. But I had a bigger problem.

"Excuse me. None of these have locks."

The guard shrugged. "They broke. Nothing much we can do."

I looked inside my purse, which held my wallet with all my money for the trip and my phone. I was hesitant to leave it, but I didn't see any other choice. Visiting hours would be over soon, and I needed to talk to Walker.

I took out a piece of gum, popped it into my mouth, and chewed it for a few seconds. Then I smushed it into the lip of the frame before stashing my purse inside and closing the door firmly. I yanked the handle to check my handiwork. The gum gave a measure of resistance. Someone could still open the locker, of course, but I hoped the pink glob would be just enough of a deterrent.

"Okay," I said. "I'm ready."

The guard led me down the hall to a room with

a row of tables lining the middle. It was just like I'd seen in movies. There were chairs on both sides, with a thick glass barrier extending straight down the center. Visitors sat on one side, prisoners on the other. Telephones on either side made communication possible.

I was a little surprised to see that the room was mostly empty. A woman was talking to a male prisoner, and though I couldn't make out what she was saying, tears were streaming down her face.

The guard led me to a seat about halfway down the row. "Wait here. The prisoner will be along soon." I didn't like how the guard referred to Walker as "the prisoner," as if he were an object and not a person.

I didn't have my phone and there were no clocks in the room, so I had no idea how much time had actually passed, but it felt as though I'd been waiting forever. Finally a guard led Walker into the room. He looked like a poor copy of the boy I'd seen in the photos at his house, like an artist had traced one of the pictures and gotten the outline right, but had missed Walker's essence. He was paler, skinnier. If I was being honest, he looked sick. It didn't help that his right eye was swollen shut, and a nasty gash cut across his left cheek. He was walking with a limp, and his right arm was draped awkwardly across his abdomen. Every step looked like it hurt.

Taking in the battered man before me, I understood why Kim had felt the need to take such extreme measures. I still didn't think what she'd done was right, but Walker clearly needed help. One year in this place looked like it had aged him ten.

Walker picked up the phone on his side, and I picked up the handset on mine.

"Who are you?" he said.

"My name is Nancy Drew. I'm a friend of your mom's." It was a stretch, but I hoped it would make things less awkward. "She asked me to help with your case."

Walker sighed. "I wish she'd stop."

"She loves you. She wants to get you out of here."

"I know, but it's pointless. I'm not going anywhere. Not till I serve every day of my sentence."

"Did you do it?" I asked.

"No."

"Well then, let me prove it."

"No offense, but you look pretty young to be a detective. I mean you look even younger than me. Why should I believe you can you help me, when my lawyer, who's like thirty and has represented hundreds of people, could barely do anything?"

"I understand that you've been let down a lot, but my age can be an advantage. People underestimate me, so they drop their guard. Besides, what do you have to lose? I just need fifteen minutes of your time, and it doesn't appear that you have anything better to do right now."

Walker shrugged. I wasn't sure I'd convinced him, but at least he wasn't leaving.

"All right. What do you want to know?"

"Walk me through what happened the day of the burglary. I know it was a long time ago, but try to be as detailed as possible. There might be something someone overlooked that will help me."

"I was really tired. I'd been up super late the night before, working on a paper for my American Literature class. The professor was one of my favorites, and I really wanted to impress him. Work that day had been tough. Everyone could see I was dragging. My plan had been to go home as soon as my shift ended, shovel some food in my mouth, and pass out. I was hoping to sleep for twelve hours, minimum."

"And you told the people you worked with about your plans?"

"Yeah," Walker said. "It was a Friday, so we were talking about our weekends."

I nodded. "So anyone you worked with would have known you wouldn't have an alibi that night."

"Yeah."

"Okay. Tell me about your coworkers."

"Forever Diamonds is a pretty small place. There were only three of us, plus the owner. That day I'd been working with Ruby. Mr. Bowen, the owner, was in the back office going over the books, or something like that. I barely saw him. Out front, things were pretty slow, so Ruby and I were chatting to pass the time. Nothing out of the ordinary. She was complaining about her student loans."

I perked up. "Ruby had money trouble?"

"I don't know if 'trouble' is the right word. She was stretched thin. She'd just graduated and had a mountain of debt, so she was doing everything she could to pay it off as fast as possible. Forever Diamonds wasn't her only job. She also babysat and drove for a car service."

"So would you say Ruby had motive, then?" I asked.

"Yeah, more than I did, anyway. Frankly, that was the thing that really annoyed me about the police and lawyers. Out of everyone, I had no reason to want to steal the jewelry. I was living at home for free. My mom was paying my tuition, so all I needed to pay for was food, gas, and my phone. I wasn't getting rich working at Forever Diamonds, but I was making enough to live, and even have a little fun, you know what I mean?"

I nodded. I really wished I'd been able to bring in my notebook or phone so I could take notes.

"What about your other coworker? Were they having any money problems?"

"Henry? I don't know. He's a nice guy, but he almost never talked about himself. When we worked the same shift, our conversations were always about the Orioles or whatever movies were showing. We worked together for over a year, and I couldn't tell you where he grew up, how many siblings he has, or whether he'd even gone to college. It didn't seem like he lived lavishly, though. He'd bring lunch from home every day. He never went out to a restaurant or ordered food with us. But I don't know what was going on in his life." Walker paused, and his expression, which had been bored as he rattled off information he'd probably provided a dozen times, suddenly shifted. "There was one weird thing, though."

"Oh?" I leaned forward.

"Henry came into the store that day."

"Why was that weird?"

"He wasn't scheduled to work. We liked our jobs— at least I did—and even though we all complained, everyone seemed pretty happy there. Forever Diamonds was a good place to work, but it wasn't like we just came in and hung out on our days off. Henry said he was dropping in because he wanted to pick up his check, but that's also strange, because he was working the next day."

"Hmm. So maybe he did have money troubles?"

"Yeah, maybe."

Walker leaned back in his chair. His eyes were brighter and more focused than when I had arrived, and he was gesturing with his hands more freely, like some energy was coming back to him.

"What about the owner? How was the store doing?"

Walker shook his head. "Mr. Bowen was always pretty private about those numbers. I don't think it was doing great, but I don't think sales were so bad that he was looking at closing the doors or anything. But if you're trying to find a motive, Mr. Bowen had a solid alibi. I didn't know at the time, but he tripped at home that evening and got a concussion. He spent the night at urgent care."

"Great. That's very helpful. Is there anything you can tell me about the diamond rings that were stolen?"

"Well, they were actually from a new ring designer. Mr. Bowen had never bought from them before. They were supposed to appeal more to the younger crowd. The pieces were kind of funky—in a good way—made for people who wanted to express their personality through their engagement rings. Lots of floral settings with inset diamonds and some cool geometric shapes, but also some even weirder ones, like one was shaped like a cat's paw, and there was even an octopus. Mr. Bowen only bought the one case. He wanted to see how well they sold. We were making a special display for them, and it wasn't ready yet, so they hadn't even gone out on the floor. They'd been in their bright yellow case in the safe for a week. Oh, that was the other thing. This jeweler used bright yellow cases instead of the usual black or blue ones. Everything that company did was advertising that they were different."

"Wait. Wouldn't it be hard for the thief to resell the diamonds if they were that distinctive?" I asked.

Walker shrugged. "Not really. The diamonds themselves weren't unique. It was the shapes of the settings that set these rings apart. The thief could just pop the diamonds out and they'd be good to go."

I nodded. "What about the security system? The police built their investigation around the fact that the alarm was turned off using your code."

Walker brought his fist down onto his thigh with a loud smack. My eyes widened, and I reached my hand out instinctively, even though I couldn't touch him through the glass. Across the room, the guard eyed Walker, and I worried that if he got any more agitated, our meeting would be cut off and Walker would be whisked back to his cell. "I'm almost done," I murmured. "Just stay calm."

"Sorry. That whole thing just makes me so angry. The police acted like my code was this smoking gun leading them straight to me, but it was nothing."

"I don't understand."

"Everyone knew my code. Mr. Bowen had master access to the alarm and could get anyone's code. Once when Henry was opening, he forgot his code and got locked out of the system trying to remember it, so he texted me for mine. And one day Ruby was bored, so she tried to guess all our codes based on what she knew about us. She figured mine out in under five minutes. It's my dad's birthday, so it wasn't super hard to work out."

Walker slumped back in his seat, hanging his head. The energy I'd seen moments before was gone again.

"It just feels so unfair. No one even bothered trying to find out what really happened."

I leaned toward the glass. "It is unfair. The police should have investigated more thoroughly. Still, I hope I can do a better job than they did."

I asked Walker a few more questions, but soon enough, a guard appeared behind Walker's chair. "Time's up," he grunted.

Walker stood. "Thanks, Nancy," he said before hanging up the phone. "I appreciate you trying, even if I don't think you'll get anywhere."

As I watched him walk away, I realized what I'd

said was true: the police and Chad Ford hadn't given Walker a fair shake. He deserved better. Proving his innocence wasn't just about saving my dad anymore. Walker needed someone on his side.

As I collected my purse, I vowed that I'd do everything I could to discover the truth.

~

CHAPTER EIGHT

A Ruby among the Diamonds

I MET UP WITH GEORGE AND BESS AT A coffee shop halfway between the prison and Forever Diamonds. I was ecstatic when I saw an iced coffee with the exact amount of milk I liked already sitting on the bright pink table.

"Thank you so much," I said.

"We figured you'd need it," Bess said, smiling knowingly.

"I really do." After slipping into an empty chair, I

quickly filled them in on everything I'd learned.

"I hate to agree with the woman who kidnapped your father, but Kim's right. It really feels like the police jumped to a sloppy conclusion in this case," said Bess.

"It won't be the first time Nancy solves a case the police can't," George chimed in, before taking a sip of her own drink.

"Let's not get ahead of ourselves," I said. "I haven't solved this thing yet. What did you two learn at Forever Diamonds? Did you talk to Mr. Bowen? What's he like?"

Bess pulled out her notebook. "We didn't get to talk to Mr. Bowen. It turns out he sold the store last year, not long after the robbery. But we were able to grab a few minutes with Mr. Erickson, the new owner."

"Yeah," George added. "Apparently, it really freaked Mr. Bowen out that one of his employees stole from him. He thought he'd been a good judge of character and prided himself on it, so when he got Walker so wrong, he took it as a sign that it was time to retire."

"What about the employees there? Did Mr. Erickson keep on Ruby or Henry?"

Bess shook her head. "When he took over, he laid everyone off and brought in his own people. Even though there was nothing to suggest Walker had an accomplice, Mr. Erickson didn't want to risk it, especially since the diamonds were never found."

I sighed. It would have been a lot easier if at least one suspect was still involved with the store. One less person to track down. I guess luck wasn't on my side.

"All right. Let's start by finding the suspect with the best motive. I'm split between Ruby and Henry, but I'm not ready to eliminate Mr. Bowen, either, even if his urgent care alibi is pretty solid."

"I vote for Henry," George said. "He was super private about his personal life, and he broke his routine by coming into the store on his day off. It's like he knew something was going to go down. And if he wanted his check, he probably needed money."

"But all we have on Henry is that he dropped by the store unexpectedly," I countered. "That's hardly a crime. On the other hand, Ruby needed money. According to Walker, she was always talking about her student loans and the jobs she was working to pay them off. That's a clear motive."

"I'm with Nancy," Bess said. "Henry sounds a little odd, but we know for a fact that Ruby needed money. And those stolen diamonds were worth a million."

"Ruby it is," George said. "Did you get a last name for her? We can try to find her on social media."

"Yeah, I pulled up some newspaper articles about the case in the car on my way here and found the names of Walker's coworkers." I took out my phone and found one of the articles. "Here we go. Ruby's is Wojciechowski."

"Bless you," George said.

I laughed. "I wasn't sneezing. That's her name." I spelled it out.

"The good news is that there's probably only one person in Baltimore with that name," Bess joked.

I couldn't help giggling. "That's what I was think-ing too."

"And you would be correct. I have her Instagram."
George tapped a few times on her screen. "Let's see
what we can learn about Ruby's life. Hopefully, she's
listed where she works now." George placed her phone
in the middle of the table, and Bess and I pulled our
chairs around so we could see the screen.

George started scrolling. Right away, I learned that
Ruby had two cats: a friendly black one and a shy tabby.
She wore a lot of floral patterns, got her nails done in
fun new seasonally appropriate colors every few weeks,
and liked to post about what she ate for lunch. But
there was nothing to indicate where she worked or how
we could find her.

"Does she have any other social media accounts?"
I asked.

George shook her head. "I already looked. They
were all locked."

I picked up the phone and started scrolling again
from the top. There had to be a clue in there. We must
have missed something.

Scrutinizing the photos again, I began to notice

a pattern. While Ruby posted a lot of lunch photos, they were generally of the same three meals: a chicken Cobb salad, a falafel wrap, and carne asada tacos.

"I think I might have something. She seems to rotate through the same three lunch places every week. They're probably from restaurants near where she works. If we can figure out where restaurants that serve Cobb salad, falafel, and tacos are in a small radius, we could at least narrow down the neighborhood."

"Let me see," Bess said. I handed her the phone and she studied the photos closely, her eyes narrowing in concentration. "Nancy, take a look at this." She zoomed in on each of the three photos, pushing past the food and focusing on the tables. It took me a second to realize what she was showing me, but when it clicked, I couldn't unsee it. "The table is the same!" In each image, no matter what the food was, the table was purple with a wooden edge.

Bess nodded, excited. "I think she's eating at a food court. There would be a variety of food options, but only one kind of table."

"Like at a mall," I said, grinning. "George, how many malls are there in Baltimore?"

But I didn't even need to ask. George had taken back her phone and was already looking up the answer. "Three! The Galleria, the Shoppes, and the Plaza."

"Let's each take a mall, look at the online directories, and see if the food court has the three types of restaurants we need."

"Okay, Nancy you go to the Galleria. Bess, the Shoppes. And I'll take the Plaza," suggested George.

We worked in silence for a few minutes.

"No Mexican place at the Plaza," George said.

"No falafel at the Shoppes," Bess added.

The food court at the Galleria was large. I had found a place to get salads and a Mexican place. The falafel was the wild card. With Bess and George striking out, I really hoped the Galleria would come through. Otherwise, we were back to square one.

"Pita Pete's! Bingo!" I yelled a little too loudly. Customers at the other tables turned to look at us curiously. "Sorry," I said, my face pink. "The Galleria has all three restaurants."

George called us a car from her app, and twenty minutes later we were standing at the entryway to the Galleria. Air-conditioning blasted while Muzak poured fuzzily from the speakers. I looked up at the escalators ferrying a handful of people between four floors. This place was huge, but mostly empty.

"When's the last time you were in a mall?" I asked.

George wrinkled her brow, thinking. "At least two years ago. I order everything online."

"I still go once in a while," Bess said. "There are some clothes I like trying on before I buy them. But you're right. It's pretty rare."

"Yeah," I agreed. "I think the only time I've been recently was last year when a birthday present I ordered for Ned got lost in the mail and I needed a replacement fast."

"I wonder if malls will even exist in a few years," George said. "I think a lot of them are going bank-rupt."

I shook my head, refocusing. "We're not here to predict the future of shopping. We need to find Ruby."

"Where should we start?" George asked. "It's way past lunch, so I don't think it will work to stake out the food court."

Bess pointed across the way to a store called Jay's Jewelry. "Maybe we should start with jewelry stores. She had past experience, so maybe she got a job at one of them." It wasn't a great plan, but I was running out of ideas.

"It's a start," I said, shrugging.

"We'll find her, Nancy. Don't worry," Bess said with a smile. I appreciated her positivity.

We headed to Jay's Jewelry. As we got closer, I saw that there was only one woman behind the counter, and it wasn't Ruby.

"Maybe she's on break or isn't working today," said Bess hopefully.

"Let's find out."

We walked up to the salesperson, and I flashed her a big smile. As she stood a little straighter, now that she had prospective customers, I noticed that her name tag said AMANDA. "Hi!" I said brightly. "Is Ruby here?"

Amanda's smile fell. "You're at the wrong store. Ruby doesn't work here."

"I am so sorry. I was here at the mall last week, and Ruby was helping me pick out some earrings for my mom. It's her fiftieth birthday, and I want to get her something special. I could have sworn this was the store."

"As I said, Ruby doesn't work here," Amanda said flatly, "but I would be happy to help you pick something out."

"It's just that Ruby had already found two pairs of earrings I loved. I wanted to think about which to choose, and my friends came with me today to help me decide." George and Bess gave a little wave behind me. "One of them has to go to work soon, so I don't have time to start the whole process all over again."

"My boss is really strict about us being on time," Bess chimed in with an apologetic smile.

"I know it's awkward, but do you think you could

let me know where I can find her? Clearly, I'm all turned around."

Amanda stared at me blankly, but then her expression suddenly shifted. "This would be like a favor, right?"

I nodded. "Yeah."

"Okay, I'll tell you, but only if you do one for me in return."

"What did you have in mind?"

She reached behind her and pulled out a small rectangular sheet. "Fill out this comment card and tell my boss how great I was helping you. My performance review is next week, and I'm hoping to get a raise. This isn't the first time Ruby has won customers from me, but at least this time I can get something out of it."

"Sure." I quickly filled out the form, praising Amanda as the most helpful salesperson I'd ever encountered. Amanda seemed pleased as she slid the card into the box for customer feedback.

"Ruby's over at Diamond Deluxe. It's on the third floor."

"Thanks!"

"Good luck with the raise," George called out as we left.

We raced up the escalator and weaved through shoppers as we made our way to Diamond Deluxe at the other end of the mall.

I paused to catch my breath. Through the doorway, I saw the woman I'd seen on Instagram behind the counter, wiping down one of the display cases. "There she is! We found her."

"Go team!" George cheered, pumping her fist.

Ruby looked up and smiled. "Can I help you ladies? Scoping out engagement rings for the future, perhaps?"

"Not exactly," I said. "I'm a friend of Walker Johnson's."

Ruby's smile disappeared and her hands began to twitch. "Let me guess. You think he's innocent."

"I'm investigating the possibility, yes."

"Well, I'll tell you the same thing I told his mom."

George took a step closer. "You know Kim?"

"No, but she's written me a gazillion letters asking me to come forward and speak out on Walker's behalf. I don't think she'd really want that."

"Why not?" I asked.

"Because Walker's guilty," she said, and turned away, busying herself with straightening some papers.

"The evidence we've heard against him seems to have a lot of holes in it," Bess interjected. "What do you know that makes you so sure?"

Ruby sighed. "The afternoon of the burglary, I found Walker checking out the safe. We all had the code, just in case, but if you weren't opening or closing the store, employees didn't go in there. I asked him what he was doing, but the answer he gave me was pretty vague. I considered Walker my friend, so I didn't say anything to Mr. Bowen. If I had, maybe I could have stopped the whole thing. Looking back, I'm pretty sure Walker was doing reconnaissance."

Sweat had broken out on the back of my neck. This was the last thing I wanted to hear.

Ruby was shifting from foot to foot, casting worried glances over her shoulder. I could tell she wanted us to leave, but I had one more question.

"Have you kept in touch with Henry?"

"No one's kept in touch with Henry," Ruby scoffed. "He basically disappeared off the face of the planet not long after the robbery."

I raised my eyebrows. "And you didn't think that was odd?"

She shrugged. "Henry was an odd guy. Look, my shift is almost over, and I have to go. I have another job I need to get to, and I can't be late. But can I give you some advice? Don't waste your time on this old news. Walker stole the diamonds, and now he's in jail where he belongs. Justice was served. Just because his mom is in denial doesn't mean you need to get sucked into her delusions."

Too late, I thought. I forced a smile onto my face. "Thanks for your help. I'll keep that in mind."

Ruby darted to the back, and George, Bess, and I headed outside. I had formed my own opinion of

Ruby, but I wasn't sure if my concern for my dad's well-being was making me biased. "What do you guys think? Is what she said true?"

"Something seemed off to me," Bess replied. "She seemed really nervous and jumpy."

"And really defensive about Walker's guilt." George rubbed her chin. "She didn't even think it was worth asking whether he actually did it."

I was glad that Bess and George had picked up on the same red flags I had. "We should take what she said about Walker going into the safe seriously, but I don't think she was being completely straightforward with us."

"There she is," hissed George, pointing down a hallway that led to bathrooms and a water fountain. "The store must have a back exit down there." Ruby turned right at the end of the corridor.

"Let's follow her," I murmured. "Maybe we'll find out why she was so eager to get out of there."

Inside the mall, there were just enough people that we could stay on her trail without being spotted, but out in the parking lot was a different matter. We had to hang way back and eventually we lost her.

"Well, that didn't get us anything new," I said with a sigh.

"This might not be the time," George piped up, "but I saw a froyo place on the second floor, and I could really go for a chocolate swirl with peanut butter if they have it. Or maybe they have cheesecake. . . ."

Suddenly a BMW convertible screeched past us.

"Bess," I yelled as the car careened toward her.

Bess leaped back just in time. "Was that Ruby at the wheel?" she asked, catching her breath.

"It sure was!" George cried. "Are you okay?"

"I'm fine," Bess said, brushing herself off. "That was quite the ride!"

"Yeah," I agreed. "She was driving a really nice car."

"Didn't Walker say Ruby had a mountain of student debt? And we know she's still working multiple jobs," George asked. "How could she afford a car like that?"

"I have one idea," I said. "It's clear and sparkly and highly coveted."

~

CHAPTER NINE

Hollywood Calling

"DID EITHER OF YOU GET HER LICENSE plate?" George asked. "I bet I could track down when she bought the car and we could see if the timeline matches the robbery."

"I think I remember an eight-two-three . . . ," Bess said.

"Wait. Stop."

"What is it, Nancy?" Bess looked concerned.

"We need to take a step back. The only reason we think Ruby is in debt is because Walker told us she was. For all we know, he's not telling the truth."

I sat down on the curb and took a deep breath. It felt like I was being pulled in a million directions, and I needed to slow all the thoughts bouncing around in my head. George and Bess lowered themselves to perch on either side of me.

"I've been approaching this case all wrong," I said, shaking my head. "I wanted to prove Walker was innocent because I was sure that was the best way to help my dad."

"It is," insisted George.

"Maybe, but that's not how you solve a case. If I'm following an agenda, I'm no better than the police. They wanted Walker to be guilty because it was easier for them. I'm doing the same thing."

Bess put her hand on my shoulder. "I think you're being a little hard on yourself. This isn't a normal case."

"I know. Even so, we should be following the clues to see where they lead. I need to be more objective."

"What do you want to do?" George asked.

I was silent for a moment, considering my options. I needed to hear what had happened from someone who wasn't as invested in the outcome. "I want to talk to Mr. Bowen. He's the victim of the crime. Ordinarily, that's who I would start with, and I want to hear his version of the events."

Bess gave a sharp nod. "Let's talk to him, then."

"I sure hope he's easier to find than Ruby was."

"Oh, he will be," George said, giving Bess a wink.

I looked back and forth between them, and it slowly dawned on me why they both looked so smug. "You got his number from Mr. Erickson when you were at Forever Diamonds, didn't you?"

Bess grinned as George polished her nails against her shirt. "We got his address, too."

"We figured you'd probably want to talk to him at some point," Bess added.

"I couldn't do this without you two."

I punched the number into my phone as George read out the digits. It went straight to voice mail, but I was ready.

"Ben Bowen? This is Nancy Drew. I'm a film producer out in Hollywood. I recently read an article about your store being robbed by your employee. I thought it might make a good movie. I don't want to speak out of turn, but I know Tom Hanks is looking for his next role, and when I saw your picture in the paper, I thought he might be perfect to portray you. I'd love to talk to you about it and see if we can work out a deal. Please call me back at this number when you get a chance."

As soon as I hung up, we all broke out in giggles. It felt good. I hadn't laughed this hard since before I'd noticed the missed calls from my dad.

"You're a genius, Nancy," George said, trying to catch her breath. "How did you even come up with that?"

I shrugged. "I didn't want Mr. Bowen to know I'm a detective. I think I made a mistake by telling Ruby too much. After all, there's only one person I could be working for: Walker. And if people really think he did it, they're not going to want to help get him out of jail."

"How did you know Mr. Bowen looks like Tom Hanks?" Bess asked.

"I don't. I just figure anyone would be flattered to hear that Tom Hanks was interested in playing them in a movie."

"I think you're right. I bet Mr. Bowen calls you back in the next thirty seconds."

Right on cue, my phone buzzed. "It's him. George, you're psychic." She smirked, looking, if possible, even more puffed up. I shook my head, taking the moment to focus before accepting the call.

"Hello?"

"Is this Nancy Drew? This is Ben Bowen. I got your message."

"Mr. Bowen, hi. Thanks for calling me back. As I said, I'm interested in developing a movie about the robbery at your store. I'd love to hear more about your experience."

"Yeah, I was very excited by the idea of Tom Hanks. But I gotta ask, what makes you think this would be a good movie? It seems pretty straightforward to me."

Mr. Erickson had told George and Bess that Mr. Bowen felt betrayed by Walker stealing from him. I could use that. "I'm more interested in the psychological facet of betrayal. My understanding is that the young man who committed the robbery was one of your employees. That must have been tough."

Mr. Bowen sighed. "You have no idea. I thought Walker was the one I would hand the store over to when I decided to hang up my jeweler's loupe. Frankly, this whole incident was like getting stabbed in the back by my own son."

My eyebrows shot up. Based on what Kim and Walker had said, I'd thought this job had been temporary—something Walker did to pay the bills while he was in college.

"Oh, really? Why's that?"

"I hadn't met someone with his kind of passion for diamonds . . . well, since I developed my own interest in them. He knew about cuts. About the business. He had all these ideas about how to make diamond mining fair for the workers. I'm sure you've heard that diamond sales have taken a hit as more and more people learn about the terrible conditions workers are subjected to in the mines. Walker had a genuine fondness for the stones. He told me had a list of the pieces he'd buy if he ever struck it rich. I guess he couldn't wait that long."

Mr. Bowen was quiet. I was a little surprised by the intensity of his emotions after so much time had passed. If I didn't know better, I'd have thought the robbery happened last week.

After a moment, I heard Mr. Bowen's breathing even out, so I pushed forward with my questioning.

"If we turn this whole affair into a movie, we'll have to have some other suspects. Red herrings, if you will. Could you tell me anything about your other employees? Would any of them have had a motive we could explore? For instance, I heard Ruby had significant debt."

Mr. Bowen burst out in a guffaw. That certainly hadn't been the reaction I'd been expecting.

"Mr. Bowen?"

"Sorry. That's rich, forgive the pun. Ruby doesn't have a lick of debt."

"She doesn't?"

Mr. Bowen broke out in another peal of laughter, though he managed to get control of himself more quickly this time. "Ruby's the daughter of one of the biggest gem importers in the world. The clue's right there in her name: *Ruby*."

I was confused. "Then why would people think she was so hard up?"

"Well, I don't think she wants people to know who she is. She used that ridiculously long last name as an alias. I assumed she was trying to make herself more relatable to her coworkers, you know? Keep things from being awkward."

"If she's the daughter of one of the biggest gem importers in the world, then why was she working as a salesperson at Forever Diamonds?"

"She was learning the business. Her dad wasn't going to hire her as an executive straight out of college with no experience. He wanted her to work in a variety of positions at different stores that bought from him. I heard she's working as a manager at Diamond Deluxe now. A few more years and she'll be on the executive track, training to become a CEO, just like her dad."

"So, just to be clear, Ruby could get her hands on any diamonds she wanted at any time?"

"Yep. I don't think Ruby is going to work out as one of your red herrings. Our other employee, Henry, would make a much better suspect."

"Oh, really? Why?"

"If anyone was in financial trouble, it was poor Henry. From what he told me, his parents died when he was a baby, and he was raised by his grandmother. A couple of years ago, she got sick. The medical bills were bankrupting them."

"How terrible." That sounded like a strong motive and a terrible experience. Even though I'd never met Henry, I felt sorry for what he'd had to go through.

"Yeah, Henry was really private. I don't think he ever told Walker or Ruby about his situation at home. I only found out because he was always asking me for extra shifts. We weren't doing enough business for me to help him much, though. I think things were getting really bad there at the end."

"Why would you say that?" I asked.

"Henry started picking up his paychecks as soon as I cut them. If he had a shift the next day but the check was ready, he'd go out of his way to stop by the store to grab it."

"Wow."

When I didn't respond right away, Mr. Bowen added, "He'd make a good suspect, right? For the movie?"

"Definitely. You know, I'd love to hear more of his story. I always think mysteries are better when all the characters are well rounded. Do you think you could give me his number?"

"Unfortunately, I lost touch with him after the robbery. He changed his number, and when I sent him a couple of e-mails to check in, they kept bouncing back. Eventually, I stopped trying."

"You don't think that's at all suspicious?"

"He was a kid who had gone through a lot. I expect he was looking for a fresh start."

I wasn't so sure, but I didn't think I was going to get much more from Mr. Bowen.

"Well, Ben. Thanks so much for your time. I'll have to run the details of our chat by my partners, but we'll be in touch soon."

After we hung up, I turned back to Bess and George and quickly filled them in.

"How are you feeling, Nancy?" Bess asked.

I bit my lower lip. "I'm not ready to write off Ruby. She was willing to lie to her friends and spin all sorts of stories about side jobs and debt when she didn't need to. It sounds to me as if she liked the thrill. And we definitely need to track down Henry. He has a motive—a good one. I'm not as convinced his disappearing act was as innocent as Mr. Bowen's making it out to be."

But before we could figure out how to track down Henry, my phone rang again.

It was my dad.

"Hey, Nancy. Just checking in."

"We're fine. Are you okay?"

"How's the case going?" he asked. I couldn't help but notice that he hadn't answered my question, and I thought I heard a slight quaver in his voice.

"Well, I have a suspect—one of Walker's coworkers. We're trying to track him down now." I thought it was better not to mention that I wasn't ready to rule out the possibility that Walker was, in fact, guilty. Dad sounded stressed enough.

A crash erupted somewhere in the background, like several dishes had been thrown to the ground. "Dad! What's going on?"

"Walker was attacked again at the prison. They're taking him to the hospital ward. Kim's a little upset, but I have it under control."

"Are you sure? That didn't sound like things are 'under control.'"

"She has to feel her feelings, Nancy. She's scared, sure, but none of her frustration's directed at me. I'm safe, I promise. I just need you to keep working the case. Find that coworker."

There was another loud crash, and then I heard Kim screaming.

"I'm working as fast as I can," I said, trying to block fear from creeping into my voice.

"I know you are, sweetheart. I'm sure you're doing an incredible job. And don't worry about me. I really do have a handle on this."

"Okay."

"Kim! Put it down!"

"Dad? What's happening?"

"Kim! It will all be fine. Put the gun down."

"Gun!" I shrieked.

"Gun!" Bess and George yelled, echoing me, before rushing to my side and leaning in to hear what was happening on the other side of the line.

"Do you want me to call the police?" George asked, giving her phone a shake.

"That will not be necessary, Georgia."

"Georgia," Bess repeated. "He's using your full name. He must be serious. I wouldn't risk it."

I waved George off, even though my heart was racing and my tongue felt like it was made of cotton.

"Dad?" I squeaked. "What's happening? Did Kim put the gun down?"

BANG!

"Dad!" I screamed.

There was no answer.

CHAPTER TEN

~

A Meeting in the Park

"NANCY, IT'S OKAY. I'M OKAY." MY DAD WAS back after an unbearably tense few seconds.

My heart was still racing, as I tried to regain control of my voice. "You have to get out of there right now! I know you want to help Kim, and I promise I'll still work the case, but it's not safe for you to stay."

"Kim scared herself when the gun went off. She's locking it in her safe right now."

"Dad—"

"Nancy, it's not up for discussion. I'm not leaving Kim all alone. She needs someone to stay with her.

She spent a lot of time overseas, and many of her local friends turned their backs when Walker was arrested. She doesn't have anyone else."

I could tell from the tone of his voice that there was no point arguing. Once Dad's made up his mind about something, he won't budge. I've been told we're very similar that way.

"Track down this new suspect. I'll take care of things here."

"Okay," I replied reluctantly, before hanging up the phone and turning to Bess and George. But I didn't need to explain. My face must have said it all.

"Let's find Henry," Bess said quietly.

I nodded, trying to refocus on the problem we could do something about. "No one disappears without a trace, right? So where do we start?"

"I have an idea," George began, "but it might be a long shot."

Long shot or not, any idea would better than where we were.

"We could Google Henry's name and see what

comes up. It'll at least give us a place to start."

I shrugged. "It's worth a try."

George typed Henry's name into her phone.

"What's that?" I asked, pointing to a result from a funeral home.

George clicked the link and an obituary for a woman named Mary Katherine McKnight came up. Henry was listed as her only surviving relative. She'd died just after the robbery. "This must be Henry's grandmother," I said, then paused as an idea took shape. "George, can you search property records for her name? Mr. Bowen said Henry had lived with his grandmother. If we can find her house, maybe we can find Henry."

"On it," George said. "Give me a minute." And then she was tapping and swiping at her screen.

"How are you holding up?" Bess asked, scooching closer to me.

"I'm okay. It's just been a really intense couple of days."

Bess nodded. "I know you're feeling stressed out,

but you've made a ton of progress. Think back to yesterday morning: you didn't even know where your dad was. Then you got a year-old case dumped in your lap, and in just a few hours, you've talked to three of the four people involved and ruled out one suspect. Honestly, you're like Super Sleuth."

"Stop," I said, smiling thinly. "You're going to make me blush. But seriously, thanks, Bess. I needed to hear that."

"Got it!" George called out. "2026 East Hudson Street. It's only a ten-minute walk from here."

Soon we were walking up the path of a light gray colonial with green trim. A large padded envelope, addressed to Claudia Buhrmaster, sat on the stoop. I picked it up and knocked. After a moment, a young woman opened the door.

"Can I help you?"

"Hi. First of all, I think this is for you," I said, handing her the package. "We're friends of Henry. We were wondering if he's home."

"I don't know anyone named Henry. Sorry."

I looked at George, confused. She shrugged and held up her phone. "It's the right address."

"Did you recently buy this house?" Bess asked from behind me.

"Yeah . . . just a few weeks ago. How did you know that?"

"Your clothes," Bess said with a smile. "I figured you were doing some work on the place." I registered that Ms. Buhrmaster was wearing overalls dotted with paint. Of course Bess, the most fashionable person I know, picked up on that detail.

Ms. Buhrmaster let out a relieved chuckle. "I haven't even moved in yet. I'm still fixing the place up. An old woman and her grandson lived here before, and they let a lot of repairs slide."

"The grandson!" I interjected. "That's our friend Henry."

Ms. Buhrmaster scrunched up her face and shook her head. "No, the guy's name wasn't Henry."

"What was it?" George asked.

Ms. Buhrmaster cocked her head, then started closing the door. "You know, I have a lot left to do today. I should probably get back to it."

"Wait," I said, throwing my arm out to block the door from shutting. "Look, he's our friend. He's had a really tough time since his grandma passed away and we're worried about him. If you can give us any information about how to find him, we'd really appreciate it."

Ms. Buhrmaster stared at me for a moment, then shrugged. "His name was Jake. I never met him, though. Everything went through the real estate agents. I'm happy to put you in touch with his broker. He should have Jake's contact information."

I smiled. "That would be great."

"Sure thing. I have his card inside. Hang on one second."

A minute later the woman handed me a glossy business card for Casey Keyser, with a photo of him flashing a bright smile. "I never talked to him directly, but my real estate agent said he was a nice guy. They'd done a lot of business together."

"Thank you so much," I said. "Good luck with your repairs."

She nodded and closed the door.

A little while later, I was on hold with Mr. Keyser's assistant, who was trying to patch me though to his cell phone.

"I'm sorry. He's not answering," the assistant said, coming back on the line. "I'm looking at his schedule. He just wrapped up an open house and should be on his way back to the office to drop off some paperwork. I can leave him a message. I'm sure he'll get back to you tomorrow."

"I was really hoping to hear from him sooner," I said, playing up my disappointment.

"It's almost five. We're getting ready to close up. Mr. Keyser will get back to you as soon as he can."

"Guess we're going to a real estate office," grumbled George once I caught her and Bess up. "You know this isn't really the trip to Washington, DC, I imagined. I thought we'd be unearthing clues in the National Air and Space Museum, which I really want to visit, by the way. Instead we've spent most of our time traipsing around Baltimore."

"Come on, George," Bess said in a soothing voice. "Get us a car. We can discuss the museums we wish we were visiting while we're on our way to Mr. Keyser's."

Traffic was brutal, and we were pulling up to the address on Mr. Keyser's card when I spotted a man exiting the building we were looking for and crossing the parking lot. I heard a few beeps and then saw the headlights blink on a car a few rows over.

"Stop!" I cried.

Our driver slammed on the brakes. "What the heck . . ."

"Sorry," I said, jumping out of the car. "I can't let this guy get away."

I double-checked the photo on the card Ms. Buhrmaster had given me. Wavy black hair, long nose; this was definitely Casey Keyser.

"Mr. Keyser!" I called, jogging over to him.

His head shot up. "Yes?"

"Hi," I said, plastering on a smile. "I'm Claudia. I bought the house on Hudson Street."

Mr. Keyser thought for a moment. "Gray Colonial, green trim?"

"That's the one."

"If there's a problem with the house, it's too late to do anything about it. The contract's been signed. The money has changed hands. And besides, you really should go through your own agent."

"No, no. The house is great. I have no regrets. I was doing some repairs and I found a beautiful diamond ring wedged behind a baseboard. It looked like it had been there for a long time. Isn't it true that the man I bought the house from recently lost his grandmother? I figure it was hers and that he might want it back."

"That's actually quite kind of you, but you could have just called my office."

I took a deep breath. "Oh, I did, but your assistant couldn't reach you, and she said you couldn't call me until tomorrow but that you were headed back to the office, and I was so excited about finding the ring and thinking about how happy it would make someone to get a family heirloom back that I just couldn't wait." After another breath, I launched in again. "The whole way over here, I kept imagining the story of the ring. Maybe someone smuggled it into the country as they fled—"

"Right. You have a lot of energy. I can't give out client information, but if you want to leave the ring with me, I can make sure he gets it."

"No offense," I said, "but I really don't feel comfortable with that plan. Besides, then I wouldn't get to see his face when I hand it over to him. And let's be honest, that's going to be the best part."

"Fine." Mr. Keyser sighed, then took out his keys and turned back to the office. "His number's inside. I can call him and see if he'll let me share his contact info. Follow me."

"Fantastic!" I squealed. "Thank you."

George and Bess were waiting under a tree, and I shot them a quick thumbs-up before following Mr. Keyser into a small, hip office space. It was open plan except for three offices enclosed by glass doors that lined the back wall. Giant photos of gorgeous houses stamped with what I assumed were their sale prices adorned the other three walls. Mr. Keyser pointed to two stuffed chairs next to a coffee table covered with brochures. "Have a seat. I'll call Jake."

As Mr. Keyser went into one of the offices in the back, I sank into the plush seat. The chair was very comfortable.

I must have nodded off, because the next thing I knew, Mr. Keyser was shaking me awake. "Claudia. Claudia."

"Sorry! These chairs are really soft."

"They are," Mr. Keyser conceded. "You're not the first person to fall asleep in them, actually."

"That makes me moderately less embarrassed." I hoped I hadn't drooled.

"Anyway, I talked to Jake. He doesn't want me to give you his phone number, but he said he'll meet you at Singer Park in an hour. It's just a few blocks from here. I told him what you look like."

"Thank you. I really appreciate it."

"Sure thing. Just remember this above-and-beyond service when you want to sell that house and upgrade to something bigger."

"For sure. Thanks again," I said, rushing out of the office.

We had decided to walk to Singer Park. It was still muggy, but it felt nice to be out strolling in the early evening. Even taking our time, we ended up with over forty minutes to kill while we waited for Jake. George found a food cart and bought us all hot dogs, and I was glad because I was starving. George, being George, even went back for seconds.

She was just walking back, balancing her second fully loaded dog, when a small man, shorter than me, with hunched shoulders, a scraggly beard, and gentle eyes approached us.

"Are you Claudia?" he asked softly.

"I am. You're Jake?"

He nodded, and I introduced George and Bess.

Jake took one look at George's hot dog, and I could practically see his mouth watering. Bess seemed to notice too. A moment later, she asked him if she could buy him something. Jake looked taken aback but quickly agreed, and Bess hurried off to get him the food.

"Casey said you found jewelry or something at the house, and you think it belongs to me? I thought I was really thorough when I cleaned the place out. Sorry for any bother this has caused you."

Before I could answer, Bess came back with the hot dog. "Here you go, Henry."

Jake's/Henry's eyebrows shot up, and he looked ready to bolt.

"Bess!" George scolded.

Bess looked at me, her eyes wide. "I'm so sorry, Nancy. It just slipped out."

"Nancy?" Henry squeaked. "I thought your name was Claudia. This is a trap! You don't have a ring for me. Look, I don't have any money. I'm not avoiding your calls because I'm ripping you off. I literally have nothing to give you!"

"Whoa, whoa. You're partially right. I don't have a ring. But whoever you think we are, we're not them. I promise."

"Who are you, then?"

As I explained why my friends and I were so eager to speak with him, I could see Henry's shoulders relax. "Before we go any further, why are you using a fake name?"

He sighed. "Even with selling the house, I didn't have enough money to pay all my grandmother's medical bills. I changed my name and have been lying low to avoid bill collectors. That's who I thought you were."

"That sounds really hard," Bess murmured. "I'm sorry."

"It has been. Thanks." He was quiet for a moment. "I didn't know that people thought Walker was innocent."

"Well, I don't know if it's people so much as his mom," I explained. "But she's very . . . determined. And Walker's case deserves a thorough investigation, so that's what I'm trying to do."

"You know, I did think one thing was funny about the case . . . ," said Henry.

"What's that?" I asked.

"Everyone just assumed the burglary happened at night, when the security system was accessed using Walker's code."

"You don't think it was?"

Henry shrugged. "Maybe. We could access the alarm system remotely from an app on our phones. It worked within a five-mile radius of the store, but that was a bug in the system. It was only supposed to work from a few feet away. I figured it out one night when I was bored. If I figured it out, other people could have done it too."

I gaped at him. Glancing over, I saw that Bess's eyes were wide and George was biting her lip. I knew she was resisting the urge to jump in with a barrage of questions. When I turned back to Henry, his expression was impassive. I don't think he realized that he'd just dropped a bombshell into our laps. I almost laughed. This piece of information could upend the entire case, and he'd shared it with barely a shrug.

"Just so I'm sure I understand," I started slowly, "you're saying that someone could have stolen from the safe at any time during the day, and then used Walker's code to access the alarm system that night to make it seem like that was when the robbery happened."

"Exactly."

"Why didn't you say anything to the police?" George blurted out.

"I wasn't thinking clearly when they talked to me. I'd never even set foot in a police station before, let alone an interrogation room. I could barely even remember my name when I first sat down. And then once I remembered about the glitch later, Walker had already pled guilty, so there didn't seem to be any point in bringing it up. I feel terrible that keeping this information to myself might have hurt Walker."

"You brought it up now," Bess said gently. "That's the important thing."

"I just assumed that since he pled guilty, he'd done it."

"It's tough to wrap your head around," I agreed.

"And we still haven't proven that he wasn't responsible for the robbery."

"If Walker did know about the bug, though, he probably would have given himself a better alibi than being home alone asleep," George pointed out.

"That's true." I sighed. "But if our culprit did take advantage of this bug, the entire timeline we've been working with is completely off. We're back to square one."

CHAPTER ELEVEN

A Timeline Emerges

"I NEED TO GET GOING," HENRY SAID. "I'M working nights this week. Thanks for the hot dog," he added, turning to Bess.

As he walked away, I sat down on a bench and took a deep breath. *This is just a setback,* I told myself. *It doesn't mean your entire investigation has been a waste.* But there was no time to wallow. I had to figure out a way forward.

"The good news is that Walker's lack of an alibi doesn't matter anymore, I guess," remarked George. "If the diamonds weren't necessarily stolen at ten p.m., it doesn't matter that he was home asleep with no one to vouch for him."

"That's true." I perked up a little. "It also means that Mr. Bowen's strong alibi no longer lets him off the hook."

"Well, I for one think Henry is innocent," Bess said, going a little pink.

George smirked at her cousin. "You just think that because he's very sad and needs to be taken care of. You always want to take care of everyone."

"That's not true!" Bess protested.

"It is true, Bess, and you know it," I said, patting her hand. "It's something we love about you. But it doesn't mean you're wrong about Henry. He probably wouldn't have told us about the glitch in the security system if he was using it to cover his tracks. Let's cross him off our list and put Mr. Bowen back on."

"How do we feel about Ruby?" George asked.

"I'm not sure. She doesn't have a strong motive to steal the diamonds, but she certainly has shown a knack for lying. I'm not ruling her out yet."

"Why would Mr. Bowen steal from his own store?" George asked.

"I don't know," I admitted. "That's definitely something we'll have to look into more. Honestly, right now Walker seems to be the strongest suspect."

We sat in silence for a moment, contemplating what that would mean for my dad.

"So, what's the next step?" Bess finally asked.

"Ideally, we'd talk to everyone involved again and get a timeline for the entire day, not just after hours, and look for inconsistencies. But I don't know how to do that. Walker's in the hospital, so we can't reach him. Who knows where Ruby is and how long it would take to track her down again? I guess we could call Mr. Bowen again. See if we learn anything else. But that doesn't help with everyone else's timelines."

I drummed my fingers on the bench, trying to think what to do. "Actually, I do have one idea, but it's definitely a gamble."

"I think at this point, anything's a gamble,"

remarked George. "Besides, you were the one who said any idea is better than none."

"That's true. Then I think we should see what evidence the police gathered. Just because they concluded Walker was guilty doesn't mean they didn't take statements from Mr. Bowen and the others. Maybe there's something that will point us in the right direction."

Bess looked a little worried. "That sounds like a good next step, but these officers don't know us. They're not going to help us the way River Heights PD does."

"I know," I said. "That's why it's a gamble. We're going to have steal the files."

Bess and George stared at me for a moment, their eyes wide.

"Nancy . . . stealing? I don't—" George started, but I cut her off before she could try to talk me out of my plan.

"I know it's wrong. I don't like the idea of stealing either, but my dad is trapped in a house with a woman beside herself with worry, and she has a gun. To get him out of there, we need this evidence, and if I could think of another way to get it, I would do that. But I can't. Can you?"

They were both quiet. Finally, Bess shook her head.

"Me neither," George added. After a moment, George's expression settled into steely resolve. "We'll get those files, because you're right. This is about saving your dad."

Bess gave me a weak smile, then leaned in and squeezed my hand.

I still felt uneasy. I didn't like crossing this line, but if I had to do it, I was glad my friends had my back.

When we arrived at the police station, I waited to the side of the door, out of view, while Bess and George went inside.

A moment later the door swung open, almost squashing me. George and Bess were running out, a police officer on their heels.

"Come quick," George yelled, taking off down the street. "He went this way!"

"I'm really not supposed to leave the front desk," the officer called, panting.

"He's going to get away!" Bess cried. "You have to come right now!"

The officer hesitated for a second.

"Please!" Bess pleaded, widening her eyes.

"All right, let me just radio for someone to cover the desk," the officer said, rushing past me.

Without hesitating, I slipped inside. The lobby was empty apart for an old woman dozing in a chair. I crept past her, trying to make as little noise as possible.

My hand was on the doorknob to the bullpen when the woman called out, "What are you doing?"

"Just visiting my boyfriend," I said with a bright smile. "It's his first day on the job and I wanted to say hi."

The woman looked at me suspiciously, but I just kept smiling. I could feel sweat starting to bead on my forehead. I hoped I was far enough away that she couldn't see it.

After a tense moment, she leaned her head back against the wall. "Enjoy love while it lasts," she murmured before closing her eyes again.

I passed through the doorway into the bullpen of a typical suburban police station, not all that different from the one back in River Heights. The phones rang steadily, but not off the hook. There was a holding cell in the back, and a man was yelling about wanting to be let out. The officers, in uniform and plain clothes, ignored him as they milled about.

I had been in enough police stations in my time to know that evidence was usually stored in a specific room. I saw a hallway in the back that looked promising.

As I crossed the space, trying to appear as though I belonged there, I noticed a young officer looking at me quizzically. Not good. I needed to avoid being noticed if this was going to work. Just as he was making a move to get up, a woman's voice called, "Lopez! I need you in my office."

"Yes, Sergeant!" the young officer responded, forgetting about me as he hustled into see what she needed.

I hadn't made it more than twenty feet when a burly man in a suit, sporting a thick mustache, stopped me.

"Can I help you with something, young lady?"

"No, I'm fine, but thank you." I went to pass him, but he stepped to the side, again blocking my path.

"That was a rhetorical question. Let's try again. What exactly do you think you're doing?"

"Oh!" I said, as if it hadn't occurred to me that I shouldn't be here. "I'm Lopez's girlfriend. I was just dropping dinner off for him, and I needed to use the restroom before I headed home. What's your name, sir?"

The man didn't so much as break eye contact with me. I knew that if I glanced away, he'd know I was lying, so I steadied my breathing and kept looking him square in the eye, holding my smile firm. Finally, he caved. "Detective Ferreira," he replied gruffly. "It's nice to meet you." He held out his hand. "Lopez is a good egg. But he knows better than to let civilians back here."

"It's my fault. I wouldn't take no for an answer. It won't happen again."

Detective Ferreira grunted and stepped aside, and I made it to the hallway without any further interruptions.

I had to stop myself from shouting with glee when

I saw a sign that said EVIDENCE halfway down the hall.

A stern woman with curly hair and half-rim glasses sat glowering just inside the door—Eileen Flynn, if the nameplate on her desk was anything to go by.

"Hi," I said. "I'm the new intern. I just started today, and I haven't met you yet. Detective Ferreira asked me to make copies of some interview transcripts for him."

"ID?"

I started to hand over my license, but she gave me a withering look. "Your *police* ID."

"Oh, it's not ready yet."

Eileen raised her eyebrows. "They usually have those made in twenty minutes."

I shrugged. "The machine's broken." Leaning forward, I asked, "Do you think you could let me back there, anyway? Detective Ferreira is really intimidating, and I don't want to get on his bad side . . . especially on my first day."

She sighed. "Go ahead."

The room was filled with rows and rows of metal shelves piled high with file boxes. Fortunately, they were in chronological order, and I was able to find the box with records pertaining to the burglary quickly. There wasn't much inside. It seemed Kim was right— the investigation appeared to have been a hasty one. I did luck out and find transcripts of interviews with everyone associated with the store.

I was making copies when I heard Detective Ferreira's voice in the hall. "Lopez! I met your girlfriend earlier. She seems very sweet."

"Girlfriend?" Lopez said. "I don't have a girlfriend."

My stomach dropped. I had one more transcript to copy: Walker's. I needed to get those pages through the copier and get out of the station as soon as possible or I was going to be in big trouble. I shoved the pages into the tray and hit the start button a bunch of times.

"What did you say?" I heard Detective Ferreira ask, his voice low and angry.

"I don't have a girlfriend?" Lopez repeated hesitantly.

Half the pages were through the feeder. . . . "Come on. Come on. Come on," I muttered, willing the machine to go faster.

"Well, there's a redheaded girl wandering around telling people she's your girlfriend," the detective snapped.

"Oh, her? I saw that girl. I have no idea who she is."

"We need to find her ASAP!"

"Was she wearing jeans and a gray cardigan?" Ms. Flynn called out.

Finally the copies were done. I grabbed all the papers and shoved them into my bag, along with the rest of the copied transcripts.

"Yeah," I heard Detective Ferreira shout. "Have you seen her?"

I shoved the originals back in the box and hurried to return it to its shelf.

"She told me she was an intern. She's in here."

Suddenly it got really quiet. I knew that any minute, the door would swing open and I'd be trapped. My eyes darted around the room, as I searched for any possible means of escape before spotting a small window. If I could slip through it and run, I might have enough of a head start.

I was twenty feet from the window when the door

opened, and I heard three sets of footsteps and frantic whispering. Luckily, the shelving holding the evidence boxes blocked me from view.

Taking off my shoes so they wouldn't hear my footsteps, I sprinted across the room, peering up the wall as I got closer. The widow was near the top, a good eight feet off the ground. Fortunately, there was a file cabinet right under it.

I shoved my shoes into my bag and hoisted myself on top of the cabinet, all the while trying to stay quiet, but my knee banged into the side, making a loud clatter.

"This way!" Detective Ferreira bellowed. I didn't bother to look back. Flinging open the window, I threw my bag out and jumped. It was about ten feet to the ground. Fortunately, I've jumped from substantial heights before, so I knew how to protect myself.

I bent my legs slightly, making sure to land on my toes, and propelled myself forward into a somersault to absorb the impact from the fall. It had been a while since I'd practiced that move, and my knees and ankles ached, but I didn't think I'd actually injured myself.

But I didn't have time to stop and take stock, and I was pretty sure adrenaline was dulling the pain and I'd regret that stunt later.

Popping up, I raced down the block. My sock-clad feet stung as they pounded the concrete, but I couldn't risk stopping to put my shoes back on. I needed to get as far away from the police station as possible. Luckily, neither Detective Ferreira nor Officer Lopez had tried to copy my acrobatic feat. That might buy me a little time.

When I was several blocks away, I crouched down between two parked cars, trying to make my breathing as quiet as possible. After five minutes had passed and no officers had appeared, I decided the coast was clear and pulled my phone to call George.

"Meet me back at the café we went to before," I whispered.

"What?" George asked. "Where are you, Nancy? Why are you whispering? Are you okay?"

"I'm fine, but we need to get away as fast as

possible. We shouldn't waste time meeting up here. It's too risky. I'll explain everything at the café."

"Okay, got it. See you soon. And you're buying my coffee."

I put my shoes back on and pulled up the app to call a ride.

As the car sped away ten minutes later, I finally felt like I could relax. That had been way closer than I would have liked.

Bess and George arrived moments after me. I quickly caught them up on my escapades inside the police station, then handed out the transcripts while George got us coffees and snacks.

"Okay, start reading," I said when George returned. "There are four in all, so whoever gets done first can work on the last one. Mark anytime someone says they went into the safe. Anything weird, anything inconsistent, make a note."

Then we got to work.

I'd grabbed Walker's transcript, and I didn't see

any major deviations from what he'd told me at the prison. That was a good sign. According to his testimony, he'd gone into the safe around two thirty p.m. to switch out one of the diamonds in the display case. That must have been when Ruby saw him. It didn't explain why he'd been cagey when she asked what he was doing, but I was glad to see that he'd at least acknowledged it.

As I turned the page, Bess grabbed the extra transcript and started scribbling notes.

A few minutes later, when we were all finished, I yanked out my notebook and flipped to a blank page. As I grabbed my pencil, I realized my hand was shaking. We were so close. I could feel it.

"Okay, let's start by making a timeline of when the safe was opened. The thief couldn't have gotten the diamonds without going into the safe, so maybe knowing exactly when the door was opened will give us a clue. Bess, do you want to go first?"

"Sure. So let's talk about Henry. Since he only stopped by to pick up his check, he didn't go into the safe at all. I really think we can mark him as innocent."

"I agree. There's nothing that points to him as our culprit."

Bess smiled, then continued on. "Ruby opened the store that day, so she pulled some of the more valuable pieces from the safe and put them on display. That was at eight forty-five a.m. She didn't report going back into the safe again that day."

"That matches what Walker said in his transcript," I said, writing *8:45 a.m., Ruby* in my notebook. "He was supposed to help Ruby open, but he'd been putting the finishing touches on that paper he was up all night writing and was a little late to work. When he got to the store, Ruby had taken the necessary pieces from the safe. He did go into the safe at two thirty to exchange one of the stones."

"Maybe Ruby stole the diamonds when she was all alone at the store," George suggested, excited.

"That's definitely a possib—" I suddenly remembered something Walker had said in the prison.

"What is it, Nancy?" Bess asked, but I was so

focused on replaying my conversation with Walker, I didn't answer right away.

"Earth to Nancy!" George teased.

I shook my head. "Sorry. Walker told me that the stolen rings were in a bright yellow case, which is unusual in the jewelry trade. If Ruby had stolen the rings that morning, anyone who went into the safe after her would probably have noticed they were missing, and that includes Walker. I don't think the diamonds were taken before two thirty."

Bess furrowed her brow. "If the case was so distinctive, then the last person who went into the safe probably is the thief. Otherwise, anyone who opened the safe after the theft would have noticed it was gone."

"Yeah," I said, "Or they really were stolen later that night."

Bess and I both turned to George.

"Mr. Bowen went into the safe twice," George said. "Once at eleven thirty a.m., and"—she paused dramatically—"once at five thirty when he closed the store."

My thoughts were racing. "George, what urgent care clinic did Mr. Bowen go to? Does the transcript say?"

"Let me see," George said, flipping through the pages in her hand. "Ah, here it is. Speedy Care on Frederick Road."

I yanked out my phone and pulled up my maps app, then typed in *Speedy Care* and *Forever Diamonds*. "The clinic and the store are just under four miles apart. That's within the distance Henry said they could access the security system remotely. Mr. Bowen could have grabbed the case of diamonds as he was closing the store, waited a few hours, gone to urgent care claiming to have fallen, and then accessed the security system from the clinic using Walker's code, giving himself an alibi and framing Walker in one fell swoop."

"That would work," George said. "And it's a way better theory than Walker being dumb enough to use his own security code to commit a major crime."

"Do you think it's enough, Nancy?" Bess asked.

"I don't know. I agree that it's a good theory, but that's all it is. We don't have solid proof."

"Maybe you should call your dad and ask," George suggested.

I nodded and pulled up Dad's number in my contacts. He answered on the first ring, and I barely said hello before launching in, racing through everything we'd learned about the security system and explaining the timeline we'd just built from the transcripts.

"That's amazing work, Nancy," Dad said as I finished.

"I know it's not indisputable proof. . . ."

"It's enough," Dad said firmly.

"It is? Are you sure?"

"Yes. Take the evidence you've gathered to Chad Ford. There's enough there to cast doubt on Walker's guilt. He can go back to the police and demand they investigate Mr. Bowen. When they find the diamonds or get a confession, Walker will be freed."

I felt my stomach sink. Dad's plan still required several more steps, and it was far from a sure thing.

"That's not the deal we made with Kim. . . ."

"I won't let you endanger yourself by confronting Mr. Bowen," Dad said firmly.

I chuckled. "It wouldn't be the first time I faced down a suspect."

"Nancy, this isn't up for discussion. Go back to the hotel and find Chad Ford. I'll explain the situation to Kim. You are not confronting Mr. Bow—"

"Did you just hang up on your dad?" George asked me, her eyebrows high.

"He said the matter wasn't up for discussion, so I decided not to discuss it."

"Wow. I think I'm genuinely shocked," Bess said.

"Me too." I gave her a small smile.

My phone buzzed. I knew it was Dad, so I was tempted to let it go to voice mail, but I couldn't do it. "Look, I'm sorry I hung up, but you asked me to trust you earlier. Please trust me now. I can do this."

He sighed heavily. "I know you can. Just . . . be careful."

"I will. I love you. I gotta go."

I hung up and turned to my friends. "We're going to Mr. Bowen's house, and we are getting our indisputable proof."

CHAPTER TWELVE

Moment of Truth

GEORGE FOUND MR. BOWEN'S ADDRESS IN her notes, and ten minutes later we were in a car headed to his house.

We rode in silence as I worked through various plans to get the confession we needed. My heart was beating fast and my breathing was shallow. If this didn't work, I didn't know what our next move would be.

"I have an idea," George said suddenly. "Bess, do you have your earbuds with you?" Bess nodded. "Give them to me." Then she turned to me. "Give me your phone."

Bess and I did as we were told. George pulled at her own phone and earbuds. After a moment, she handed me back my cell and one of Bess's earbuds. "Here, put this in your ear."

Once it was in, George placed one of her earbuds in her ear and handed the other to Bess, then tapped on her screen to call me. "I know it makes more sense for you to go in there alone, but now Bess and I will be able to talk to you, and we'll be able to hear your conversation through your phone. It's not a wire like the police use, but it will work in a pinch. Just keep the speaker pointed at Mr. Bowen."

"Great idea, George."

"Hang on," Bess said as she leaned across her cousin. "Let me fix your hair so he won't see the earbud." She pulled a bobby pin out of her own hair and strategically secured a lock, keeping it firmly fixed over my ear. "There," she said. "He'll never know it's there."

We pulled up to the house. After the rideshare car drove off, I rang the doorbell, while George and Bess hid behind a tree. I found it reassuring that they were close by, even if they were out of view.

"I'm not buying any more Girl Scout cookies!" Mr. Bowen yelled through the door.

"Oh, hi," I called back. "I'm not a Girl Scout. I'm Nancy Drew. We spoke on the phone earlier about the movie."

The door opened a crack and Mr. Bowen peered out. "I thought you were in Los Angeles."

"I'm *from* Los Angeles, but I'm in Baltimore researching the story. The more I learn about what happened, the more fascinating I'm finding it. I have a phone call with some big-time executives tomorrow. I just had a few more questions I'd love to go over with you if you have a moment."

"How'd you get my address?"

"I have a *very good* assistant."

"You're welcome," George whispered through my earbud.

Mr. Bowen looked me up and down. "You seem kind of young to be a producer."

I shrugged. "People tell me that all the time. Good genes, I guess. Look, I know it's weird I popped by instead of calling again, but I really thought it would help my pitch if I saw you in person, got a sense of your essence. That way I can better communicate the vision to the executives . . . and Tom Hanks, of course."

Mr. Bowen didn't speak. He didn't move. I still couldn't see much more than one eye staring out at me. Clenching my toes in my shoes, I kept my big smile plastered on my face, waiting him out though my cheeks ached.

"All right," he finally said, widening the opening.

I saw his face for the first time. It was soft and doughy. His hair was white and tufty at the sides. He had an innocent and oblivious look to him, and for a second, I doubted his guilt. But one thing I've learned over the years is that guilty people come in all shapes and sizes, and there is no way to predict what someone is capable of.

I stepped into the entryway.

"Good job, Nancy!" Bess whispered.

Above me, one of the light bulbs in the overhead light was burned out, giving the whole place a dark and eerie vibe. Boxes were stacked on either side of the hallway, leaving nothing but a narrow path.

"Are you moving?" I asked.

"No. I just have a lot of stuff."

He turned the corner into a small den. The couch and the coffee table were covered in old mail that had never been opened, magazines, and newspapers yellowed with age. Clothes, action figures, board games, toasters, rice cookers, and other small appliances still in their boxes were scattered around the room. It felt like a storage facility for someone with a shopping addiction.

Mr. Bowen cleared a space for me on the couch and then settled into the armchair, the only clean place in the entire room.

"So . . . how can I help you?"

"Well, a couple of things. The ending to the case isn't entirely satisfactory. I mean, the diamonds were never recovered! That will never fly on the big screen."

Mr. Bowen shifted in his seat, and I noticed that his eyes went to a corner of the room behind me.

"That's true," he said after a moment.

"Now, the other issue is that audiences want a villain. The boy who was convicted, from what I read— he just doesn't seem like a bad guy."

"Well, he's a thief. Doesn't that make him bad enough?"

I nodded. "Hmm . . . You might be right, but maybe we can kill two birds with one stone. What do you think happened to the diamonds? Where do you think Walker hid them?"

"How should I know?"

"Well, if *you* were going to hide them, where would you put them? Maybe we can brainstorm and come up with a good ending for the movie."

Mr. Bowen's posture stiffened. "I have no idea," he finally said, but his eyes shifted to the corner again. I subtly turned my head, trying to zero in on what he kept looking at. The spot was piled high with junk, no different, I assumed, from the rest of the house. Still, this pile looked different, less haphazard. Deliberate. Beyond the usual clothes, magazines, and boxes that were stacked everywhere, there was a rolled-up carpet, a mirror leaning precariously against a stack of books, and an assortment of gardening tools, including a rake and pitchfork. Everything about it said *stay away*, which was exactly why I wanted to get a closer peek. If Bess and George could create a distraction to lure Mr. Bowen out of the room, then maybe I could pull it off.

Glancing up, I realized that Mr. Bowen was watching me, waiting for my next question.

"I just think it might be a *distraction* to the audience if we don't explain where the diamonds are. . . ." I hoped Bess or George would pick up my meaning. Pausing, I waited, straining for a hint that they'd heard me. There was no response.

"I really have no idea," Mr. Bowen said flatly. "I'm afraid I won't be much help solving that problem. Do you have any other questions?" He sounded impatient.

"Let me check my notes," I said, stalling. "It's really important that nothing *distract* from the resolution. A *distraction* really gets in the way of a good story. It pulls the audience right out of that movie magic."

I paused again, waiting. The line remained quiet. In fact, it was completely silent. I no longer heard my friends' whispers or breathing as they listened from outside. Glancing down at my phone, I flinched when I realized the screen was black. The battery was completely dead.

That meant Bess and George had no idea that I needed their help.

"Who are you, really?" Mr. Bowen asked. His voice sounded aggressive—mean—and his entire face had changed. He no longer looked like the old man who'd greeted me: oblivious, innocent, slightly in awe of the world. Instead his doughy face had somehow transformed into something sharp and angular. I tried to swallow, but my mouth had gone dry.

"What do you mean?" I asked, not because I thought I could keep up my charade, but because I was hoping to buy time.

"I know you're not a movie producer. No one's genes

are that good. And I'm excellent at reading people. It's one of my better skills. You've been lying to me since you said hello. Tell me who you really are."

I looked at my blank screen again. Even though George and Bess were right outside, I was completely alone. I racked my brain, trying to land on a believable explanation that wouldn't reveal the truth. My mind, like my phone screen, was a complete blank. Time to change tack.

I gave Mr. Bowen a weak smile, and then let out a shriek, before hurling myself over the back of the couch, diving for the pile behind me.

I kept screaming as I pushed the rolled-up carpet aside, hoping that George, Bess, or even a nosy neighbor would hear me. But before I could make any more progress, Mr. Bowen grabbed me from behind and shoved me to the side. My foot caught the mirror, sending it crashing to the floor. Broken glass flew everywhere.

I clambered to my feet, but Mr. Bowen was crouched low with his hands out like a wrestler, prepared to block any attempt I made at getting back to the pile. We eyed each other warily, each breathing hard.

There was a loud thud near the back of the house. I hoped Bess and George had heard my screams and were working on a way in.

Momentarily distracted by the noise, Mr. Bowen turned his head, and I seized my opportunity. Springing forward, I hip-checked him out of the way, knocking over the pile of books in the process. Behind them, sticking out in the corner, I saw a bright yellow case, just like the one Walker had said the stolen diamonds were in.

I stretched my arm out to grab it, but Mr. Bowen's arm clenched around my neck. As I squirmed, struggling to get free, my feet slid out from under me, and I fell to my knees, right on top of some of the scattered glass shards. I screamed, this time in pain, as the sharp pieces cut into my knee. I could feel the blood soaking through my jeans.

When I fell, I'd taken Mr. Bowen down with me. I heard him let out a pained grunt, but his arm remained pressed across my throat. He was stronger than he looked. He squeezed tighter, making it difficult for me to get a lungful of air. My vision was starting to tunnel, just like it had back in the hotel room, but this time I couldn't get my head below my knees. I kept flailing, struggling to break his grip, but my attempts were increasingly feeble. I was barely putting up a fight.

Where were George and Bess?

"I'm sorry, Dad," I whispered, before I slipped into darkness.

I heard shuffling and murmuring, but the sounds were so far away. Slowly, I opened my eyes. I was lying on something soft, staring up at a popcorn ceiling.

"You're awake!" Bess cried. I turned my head toward her voice. The movement made the world swim, and I quickly squeezed my eyes shut. After a moment I tried again. Bess came into focus. Behind her, Mr. Bowen was tied to a chair. There was a gag in his mouth. George was standing guard.

"Looks like you two have been busy," I said shakily.

"Well, we had to make up for leaving you on your own for so long," George said.

Bess squeezed my hand. "Sorry about that. Getting from the bonus room, where we found an open window, to here was like making our way through a labyrinth."

"So far I've found three panini presses, but no diamonds," George said. "We didn't have much of a chance to look, though. Tying this guy up took a while."

"I think I know where they are," I said. Slowly, I sat up and made my way back to the corner. I carefully brushed away the broken glass, then knelt onto the books that had fallen in the kerfuffle, wincing. The cuts on my knees stung badly, and I made a mental note that as soon as we got out of there, I needed to clean them out. Who knew what infections I might pick up from all of Mr. Bowen's clutter? I leaned forward and carefully threaded my hand through the maze of small appliances and board games until my fingers closed around the yellow box. Once I'd slowly drawn it back out through the rat's nest, I held it up and carefully pulled open the string keeping it closed. Inside were twenty or so novelty engagement rings, glistening in the light.

I grinned, collapsing back. We had what we needed to get Walker out of jail and my dad safe. When I turned around, Bess and George didn't need me to say a single word.

"Yes!" George shouted over and over again as she jumped up and down. Bess seemed equally thrilled.

"Hey, George, does your phone have any juice left?" I asked, partly because I wanted to give Dad the good news as soon as possible, and partly because I was worried that she was going to bring the whole house down.

George stopped bouncing and handed me her phone. "Thirteen percent."

I went over to Mr. Bowen and carefully untied the gag. He shook his head, but kept his lips firmly pressed together.

Dad answered the phone right away. "George! Is Nancy okay?"

"Dad, it's me," I said.

"Oh, thank goodness."

"I have someone here who has something to say to you and Kim. Can you put the phone on speaker?"

"Should I record this conversation?" he asked quietly.

"I think that's wise," I said as I turned to Mr. Bowen. "On the other end of this phone is Walker Johnson's mother. You know Walker? He's the man who is spending time in jail for a crime you committed. You're going to jail no matter what. The least you can do is tell her why you pinned it on him."

Mr. Bowen was quiet for a moment, but then he shrugged. "It wasn't personal. If it makes you feel better, I put all the employees' names inside a hat and drew one. Walker was just the unlucky pick."

Through the speaker, I could hear Kim crying. And I felt for her. Her son had undergone a terrible ordeal, and it could just as easily have happened to someone else.

"Why'd you steal them in the first place?" I asked, trying to remain calm.

"Why does anyone steal anything?" Mr. Bowen snapped.

"There are actually a lot of different reasons—" But before I could finish my sentence, the words started spilling from the previously tight-lipped old man.

"I needed the money. As you might have gathered, I have a problem." He pointed his chin at the boxes stacked everywhere. "I can't help it. I buy so many things. Things I don't need. I've tried to stop, but I can't. I found myself in serious debt. I reported the diamonds stolen and collected the insurance money. I planned to live off that as long as I could, and I figured that by the time I ran out of that money, the heat would be off the diamonds and I could sell them."

"Did you get all that, Dad?"

"I sure did. And now I'm going to make sure the police, Chad Ford, and Chad Ford's boss hear it too."

"Thank you, Nancy," Kim said. She must have turned away from the mic, but I could still hear her voice, though it was fainter. "You're free to go, Carson."

I could feel the weight I had been carrying for the

past two days lifting off my shoulders. Dad was safe. Walker would be free. I had solved my case.

George, Bess, and I hung around until the police arrived. An officer took the rings as evidence while another handcuffed Mr. Bowen. The three of us stood watching as the squad car carrying him pulled out of the driveway and rolled down the street.

An hour later, we were back at the hotel. Dad sprang for a suite, and the four of us were eating room-service ice cream sundaes when Dad's phone rang.

"Hello? This is he—Oh, that's great news. Thanks for letting me know." He hung up. "That was the new DA assigned to Walker's case. He's working on overturning Walker's conviction ASAP. And Chad Ford has been suspended, pending an investigation."

"What's going to happen to Kim?" I asked. "I know she was out of her mind with worry for her son, but she still kidnapped you and held you at gunpoint!"

Dad sighed. "I talked to Kim. She's promised to get some help and process everything she's been through.

She's seen a lot between the war and Walker's conviction. It's not going to help her or make society any safer if she's in jail. She should be home helping Walker work through the ordeal he's been through."

I bit my lower lip. It didn't seem right.

"I know you don't like it, Nancy, but justice isn't always about locking someone up behind bars. Sometimes, it's about helping them heal. Kim going to jail wouldn't make me feel any better, and I don't think I'd be able to come to terms with the fact that her accidental encounter with me ruined her life."

I looked at George and Bess. "What do you guys think?"

"I agree with your dad," Bess said.

George shrugged. "I don't know. It feels wrong for Kim not to be punished, but it also feels wrong for her to go to jail."

I open my mouth to keep arguing, but suddenly remembered the copies of the police files crammed in my bag. I could justify it however I wanted, but I'd lied my way into a police station and stolen those transcripts.

I hadn't even tried to find a way to get them legally.

My cheeks burned as a shame flooded through me, settling in the pit of my stomach. No, I hadn't kidnapped anyone, but what I had done was wrong. I'd known what I was doing at the time was wrong, and I still went forward with my plan. It felt hypocritical of me to demand Kim face punishment.

I turned back to my dad and nodded. "Okay. You're right."

Dad wrapped me in a hug. "Thanks, Nancy. I feel very lucky to have you as my daughter tonight. Not many people could have done what you did." He threw out his arms and welcomed George and Bess. "And I am very lucky that you two are my daughter's best friends. Thank you, all."

I closed my eyes. My dad was safe, my friends were by my side, and justice was being served. There was nothing more I wanted in the world.

Dear Diary,

THERE WAS STILL ANOTHER DAY OF THE conference, so we stayed in DC. While Dad attended panels and lectures, George, Bess, and I finally took in the sights.

It was hard to keep up with George at the National Air and Space Museum. She raced from one exhibit to the next. Bess led us more calmly through the National Portrait Gallery, giving us time to appreciate the paintings. When it was my turn, I picked visiting the Supreme Court. With all our talk about justice the night before, I wanted to see the highest court in the land—the place where nine people get to decide exactly what the law means.

Walking up the marble steps gave me goose bumps. I'd heard the building referred to as the Temple of Justice before, and now I understand why.

But then I remembered Walker was still behind bars for a crime he didn't commit, and the goose bumps faded.

Laws are made and enforced by people, and sometimes they get it wrong. Justice means correcting those mistakes, which is what I realized my dad was trying to do for Kim. And now that I got that, I felt fully at peace for the first time in days.